YPP-234

The New Plague

Jacqueline Druga

Special thank you to Paula, Kira and Ruth for all of your help!

Cover design by: Jacqueline Druga

To all my readers and the constant, insanely awesome support you give me each and every day.

PART ONE

THE BREACH

ONE – CALAMITY AND FEAR

PRESENT DAY

U.S. Army Biological Warfare Laboratories (USBWL)

LAB 27 – 20 miles East, Murcia, Spain

There was something about her eyes.

Katie didn't know her personally; she didn't even get a chance to know the woman's name. Their encounter was brief. Now here she was face to face in a way she never thought she'd be.

There was something about her eyes. A spark, yes that was it.

Katie focused on those eyes. There was still life showing behind them, and that crushed Katie.

The woman blinked a few times, all while focusing on Katie.

Katie owed it to her to stay with the woman, it would be wrong to look away especially when Katie was alive because of her and the life she saw would soon leave the woman's eyes.

Small spurts of blood emerged from the woman's slightly parted lips in a steady manner, perhaps with each beat of her fading heart.

She did mouth the words, 'I'm sorry' to the woman. Did the woman see? Could she understand?

Even though it wasn't Katie's fault, she felt horrible. Heartbroken, she prayed the woman wasn't suffering.

Wanting to cry and scream, Katie instead silently sobbed. Occasionally covering her mouth to quiet herself. It took everything she had to control her bodily functions from expelling, doing so would be a dead giveaway. At that moment she was well hidden under a small countertop, sandwiched between a chair and a file cabinet, hidden by the woman's fallen body.

Working for Senator Lenore James, Katie had yearly training on active shooter situations. What to do and how to handle it, but this was so much more.

This was way more than worrying about a gun.

Katie had done everything right.

Run. Hide. Fight.

The three words that Capitol Police beat into her head and others during the drills.

She didn't know if there was one, two or even more gunmen. They were right there.

How did it unfold?

Katie and four others were part of the first team to arrive, showing up in official government cars to the facility. Three senators, including Lenore, would follow in an hour.

Their visit was thrust upon the facility giving them only a half days' notice, but not giving enough time to move anything.

It wasn't what Katie expected.

It was beautiful and looked like a hotel with the exception of the large fence with a guard booth. The stucco finished, small building was welcoming with the atrium. It didn't look like a lab at all, especially one under so much scrutiny.

Led by a man who acted more like a tour guide rather than assistant director of the facility, she crossed the atrium with the others to a back doorway leading to a room with a glass observation window. Beyond that window was a lab.

The observation room wasn't small. It was long and filled with people working on computers.

"This is our upstairs laboratory," a gentleman said. "Here we work on compounds that bind. Nothing dangerous, no viruses." He led them into the lab. No one wore protective clothing or biohazard gear. It was when they were crossing the room Katie saw the woman, she sat at a desk by another door. "You'll get the in depth tour when everyone arrives, but this is a peek."

Like Katie, one of the men with Senator Morrow's office, was a first year aide, fresh from internship. Being on the trip was exciting for Katie, even though she knew she wouldn't see much.

Morrow's Aide asked, "Doesn't look very secure. What precautions do you take?"

The man smiled. "It's a very secure facility. Only one way in, one way out. Up here, there really isn't much to protect. But through here ... it's a different story." He opened the door. It led to a hallway, the walls looked like stainless steel with lights lining all the way down. It was futuristic in a way and their footsteps echoed as they walked. At the end of the hall was an elevator, next to it, a door.

Katie stepped partially down the hall away from the pack.

"Miss," the gentleman called to her. "We're going back."

Hands behind her back, Katie looked over her shoulder to him. "Is this the way to the other labs?"

He hesitated before answering. "Yes, we have a BSL4 lab below. Which is a level four virus lab. We are working on finishing it so folks like you don't have to worry about safety. It has a separate ventilation system as well. So if something breaches downstairs, it's contained downstairs. And you have to be in the system to gain access to the elevator or stairs."

Katie knew why they were there and of course, the man wasn't going to say the secret government facility was working on weapons. In fact, Katie was instructed by Lenore not to ask any questions she couldn't find answers for on Wikipedia.

The man led the group back to the door and Katie held up the rear. It was the second she crossed over the threshold that it started.

There was no mistaking the shots being fired came from the atrium. Steady shots as if whoever was firing them wasn't in any hurry.

Run. Hide. Fight.

Heart pounding, Katie kept her wits about her. Running was out of the question as she remembered the man's words.

One way in, one way out.

Did everyone else forget, because they all ran?

If they were headed toward the door, wouldn't they be running toward whoever had the gun?

Hide.

Katie had to hide. But where? Her only choice was to go in that hall and it was a dead end.

"Come on," a woman said as she rushed by, grabbing on to Katie's hand and pulling her. "This way."

'Oh, God,' Katie thought, 'we're going to the hallway?'

The woman moved fast, nearly dragging Katie to the end and to the elevator. The woman's hand was already extended towards the security panel so as not to waste time calling the elevator.

"Come on, come on," the woman beckoned after her hand was scanned.

The elevator opened and both woman jumped inside.

The woman's finger pressed desperately and rapidly on the number four until the doors began to close. The closing doors were six inches apart when Katie saw the masked man in dark camouflage enter the hallway.

Just as the doors shut, Katie heard the shot and the elevator lowered.

The woman breathed heavily. "We'll be okay down here. It's biometric. Still, we have to hide."

"Thank you," Katie said with a whimper. "Thank you so much."

She had never been so frightened in all of her life, but a part of her felt safe. The woman still held her hand, leading her. They turned a corner and there was an enormously long hall way, lined with glass windows on both side.

As they moved quickly down the hall, the woman paused briefly by each lab, pressed the exterior intercom and said, "Under attack. Shooter. Get safe."

She repeated it four more times until they reached the end of the hall. It wasn't a metal door nor was it secure. It looked like a simple wooden closet, and when they went inside, Katie saw that it was storage. Desks, file cabinets and boxes.

"Shut off your phone," the woman said, locking the door.

Katie didn't have her phone. To keep herself from being tempted to take pictures, she left it in the SUV. She watched the woman push a file cabinet toward the locked door.

"We should be safe," the woman said.

Should be. Could be.

Wouldn't be.

Katie didn't think anything about the squealing file cabinet as it scraped over the linoleum until there was a slam against the door.

Hide.

Looking left to right, Katie ducked under the cover reaching out her hand for the woman when the door blasted open.

Three gunshots and the woman dropped. She landed on her side facing Katie.

How long had she been here? Huddled under that counter, afraid to move, to breathe or whimper. Long enough to watch the woman draw her last breath and witness her eyes go dead. It took for the woman to pass away for Katie to see the name tag that was draped from around her neck and rested in a pool of blood.

Marsha.

Katie didn't feel guilty for not learning her name.

She was certain the heroic woman would rather have had Katie's attention and concern than Katie looking at the name tag.

It could have been only seconds or minutes, but it seemed like spent relentless and painful hours under that counter. Gunshots in the distance and close by rang out, they sounded calculated. She could hear screams and cries of people who tried to get away. Also the sound of glass shattering, and it wasn't just breaking sounds, it was explosives. Warning alarms buzzed and blared but were silenced. Slowing down from a vibrant horn to a whining whirl until it stopped.

How did the gunman miss Katie?

For all she knew he or she was still in that small storage room waiting for her to emerge.

Katie wouldn't. She waited. Waited for fading footsteps to get farther away and it was then she crawled out from under the counter and over to Marsha's body.

Legs wobbly and barely able to hold her up, Katie inched her way from the storage room and into the hall.

No one was there holding a gun. No one standing there waiting. Just glass and carnage. The glass was shattered and doors were blasted apart.

At the end of the hall a body lay by the elevator and another by the stairwell. Caught in the door, trying to escape, the bullet ridden torso lay just outside while the arm squeezed between the door and the jam keeping it open.

Katie knew it was a stupid move to leave and not wait for help, but it was a chance she had to take.

She saw the stairwell door as her escape, and she made her way there trying not to look at the bodies or stare too hard at the frightening sight of the destroyed labs. As she stepped through the door, she accidently kicked the arm of the man lying there and the door slammed sending a jolt of fear through her. The single emergency light did very little to help. It was dark in that stairwell and slowly, one step at a time, Katie ascended those steps.

She made it to the top, four floors up. Still no sounds, no crying.

Once in that familiar metallic hallway she aimed for the open door. The one that would lead her into the safe labs and atrium. Riddled with fear, Katie arrived at that door, peeking out first.

There on the floor was the tour guide, and next to him was Senator Morrows' aide.

Hand over her mouth, Katie whimpered and stepped over their bodies.

Don't look. Don't look, she told herself. Just get out

Once in the familiar lab room she hurried to the atrium.

Despite her best efforts not to look, Katie still saw all the bodies.

How was it possible? How was she still alive?

The openness of the atrium afforded her the chance to just run. Run as fast as she could across the blood bath area and to the freedom of outside just through the broken glass front doors. Katie knew the gunmen could be out there, she feared stepping out, to feel the relief of escape, only to be shot.

At that moment she didn't care. She rushed outside absorbing the warm fresh air hitting her with an overwhelming sense of safety.

No one was out there though. No guard, no security, no police.

No one.

Had no one called for help?

The four SUVs they had traveled in were still parked outside. The tires were flattened, windows busted.

Katie made it to the first one, the one she had been in and quietly opened the back door. On the floor was her small briefcase and she reached inside for her phone.

Relieved it was there, Katie took it to call for help. To make the call and wait for someone to show up, Katie found a safe place to hide.

TWO – CALL TO ORDER

Washington, D.C.

SIX DAYS EARLIER

Six days earlier Lenore James sat in her office. She had been a senator for thirty-seven years. A lifelong servant of the people she claimed, and played on that charm in her second bid for president of the United States. But Lenore needed more. She wasn't one of those politicians that looked for dirt on her opposition, Lenore relied on finding something all parties would praise her for. So when the frazzled looking man, nervously holding a briefcase, showed up at her office for three days straight, begging to speak to her, she quickly learned he was not a burden but rather a gift.

He had sat in the hallway just outside her office door. Lenore wasn't the first senator he tried to speak to, just the only one who didn't threaten him. Finally, she had felt sorry for him and gave him five minutes.

He didn't need much time to catch her attention. What he came to tell her, to show her, wouldn't just secure her election, it could, if true, stop a potential disaster.

Dressed in a slightly wrinkled white shirt, blue tie and brown dress slacks, the forty something man, nervously shook her hand, then swiped his long curly bangs from the rims of his glasses.

"Thank you so much," he said clutching his briefcase for dear life.

"What can I do for you, Doctor Brayden?"

"I'll cut to the chase. The Army has a weapon, one that is unbelievably scary. Something has to be done."

"And how do you know about this weapon?"

"I made it."

A part of Lenore didn't believe what Doctor Brayden told her, that perhaps he exaggerated his abilities. Lenore and others in the Senate knew about the 'supposed' secret military labs where they worked on biological weapons. Any attempt to prove it in the past was futile. When they got permission to visit a lab, by the time they got permission, if anything was there to indicate it was a military operation, the evidence was scrubbed.

They had to go secretly and unannounced.

When the information all fell in Lenore's lap it was just before primaries, and she worked on having everything come out for a nice October surprise. The process was moving along nicely and her findings could be released just in time for the elections.

Her investigation was done under the guise of needing information, which lead them to determine and investigate if any branch of the military was in fact, in violation of the Biological Weapons Policy Act of 2021.

Lenore looked like a Martyr taking time from campaigning to serve on the committee.

But not to her colleagues.

It was day eight of the hearings, and more than likely the last day.

Senator Morrow stood in her office as Lenore had her lunch. "Better hope this doesn't bite you in the ass," he told her. "You have a nice lead."

"It won't."

"Lenore, we have had twenty-eight witnesses so far. And only the minister of health from Spain confirmed anything. One man, via remote testimony."

"The media is hailing him as a whistle blower." She took a bite of her sandwich.

"We still have Doctor Brayden and General Scott from the DIA."

Morrow snickered. "You really think the Director of Intelligence is going to throw it all under the bus. And Brayden's testimony is what? His word, some rat pictures and images none of us know. Maybe his word and the minister's will make a difference to the public, but no one is going to find a violation of the policy."

"I want to have a stop placed on every one of the military's ..." she paused to do air quotes. "Bio labs that they claim are for the good. A stop, halting all operations until we can get a team in to investigate. Including Fort Detrick because you know damn well, they have something happening there."

He shook his head. "We don't."

"Why are you coming in here on my lunch break to harass me?" she asked.

"Lenore, you will get raked over the coals after the testimony finishes. I'm just watching out for you."

"I appreciate it. But I have to do this. Have you heard Doctor Brayden?"

"I read some of his facts."

Lenore shook her head. "When you hear him. You will be convinced."

"Even with Senator Oren cross examining?"

"Even then," Lenore said confidently and finished her sandwich.

Lenore sat center of the four person panel at a long table. It wasn't a huge galley as most hearings were held and shown on television. To Lenore it reminded her more of a magistrate or traffic court room.

General Scott didn't 'stand' before her, he sat at a table across from her, a few feet away. He was composed and polite. Genuinely, he seemed very honest to Lenore, which confused her because she also believed Doctor Brayden. He went down everything his department learned in the investigation.

"Does the military deal with biological and chemical agents?" he spoke rhetorically. "Yes, but studying them more on a defensive move. Other countries do have them and could use them. We need to know how to counteract them, for the safety of our men and women in the armed forces as well as civilians."

"And nothing is of an offense nature?"

"Ma'am, since you have put my department on this," he spoke. "We have looked. Being in violation of the policy means taking governments funds and using them for biological or chemical weapons. I could not find any evidence or violation."

Senator Morrows asked. "So are you saying, like the others there are no secret labs?"

"None that aren't disclosed," he replied. "So no. No secret bioweapons labs."

Senator Oren questioned. "And this USBWL, that is reportedly in Murcia, Spain. Reported by the minister there, that it is not indeed a USBWL?"

Scott shook his head. "Sir, if there is a biological weapons lab there, it is not ours."

"What do you say about Doctor Brayden testifying today?" asked Lenore.

Very calm and matter of fact, Scott answered. "I'd say you are going to hear from a disgruntled employee that didn't get what he wanted and is creating his own narrative."

"Thank you, General," Lenore said. "That will be all."

"Perhaps Senator," he added before leaving. "You need to ask him about his work with other countries. Thank you."

General Scott stood, nodded once and then left not only the table, but the room.

After he left, Oren said to the others, "Will you excuse me a moment?"

Morrows leaned into Lenore, covering his microphone. "Did you know anything about other countries?"

Lenore shook her head.

"Makes me wonder what countries."

"Bet me Oren is chasing down the general."

"Yeah. I think he is. We'll find out, won't we?" Morrows said.

Lenore heard his words, but was certain General Scott was tossing out misleading information.

When they called Doctor Joshua Brayden he looked much more together than when Lenore had first met him. She had spoken to him since, each time he seemed more nervous.

But as he sat at the table, pressed suit, haircut, he appeared a force to be taken seriously.

"Good afternoon, Doctor," Lenore said. "Can you tell us for the record who you are?"

"My name is Joshua Brayden. I am a microbiologist and with PHD in virology. I was employed for sixteen years by the United States Army Biological Weapons Program or USBWL. Originally for work at Fort Detrick, but I have moved to nine different locations during my tenure. Initially I was employed to work anthrax."

"As a weapon?" Lenore questioned.

"No, ma'am, just researching a strain that was considered resistant to treatment. We believed it to be a weapon, not ours."

"I see," said Lenore. "And how did you end up developing weapons?"

"Objection," Oren interrupted, looking over at her. "We have not established he was creating weapons. He's not stated that."

"My apologies. Doctor Brayden. Did your work progress?" she asked.

"It did. A soldier came into the hospital with a particular resistant strain. He was dying even though he had been inoculated and all treatment given." Brayden folded his hands, fiddling nervously with his fingers as he spoke. "The director at the time knew I was working on a treatable strain of Bacillus anthracis, which is the bacterium that is known as anthrax. One that was stronger than any we had seen in the lab. The soldier agreed to my unorthodox method of treatment and it worked. He survived."

Oren asked. "By unorthodox you mean you gave him another strain of anthrax?"

Brayden nodded. "It took over the previous strain and we were able to treat it. After that, I was moved to various secret locations for the creation of different weapons."

"What kind of weapons?" Morrows quizzed,

"One." Brayden lifted a finger. "My primary focus was on one weapon. Plague."

Oren chuckled. "Doctor Brayden this is not the middle ages, the plague can be treated."

Lenore looked over at Oren. "Like Anthrax?"

Brayden continued. "Bacteria is funny like that. I was told to develop a highly antibiotic resistant and contagious strain of Yersinia pestis. And that is why I am here and why I came to you, because I have succeeded. In fact, I succeeded two years ago."

"Why wait?" Morrow asked. "Why wait two years? Did you not know how bad it was?"

"I always knew how bad it was. I have seen what it does. With this strain, if we have any accidents, it's over," said Brayden. "I have tried to figure out how to stop YPP-234, but I can't. Then when I brought up my concerns, I was dismissed."

Another smug chuckle came from Oren. "YPP-234, is there a YPP-235?"

"The last is YPP-409."

Lenore gasped. "If you had it or it was so bad, why create more?"

"Like with anthrax we were trying to create a strain that could take it over, but unfortunately, YPP-234 is impervious to everything."

Morrows leaned into the microphone. "Again, why are you coming to us now? Why the two year wait?"

Brayden answered. "For the same reason I was dismissed. I wasn't dismissed over my concerns on YPP-234, I know in time

I could have beat it, but." He raised a hand slightly and dropped it in defeat. "I learned they wanted to move my work from the Murcia, Spain lab to another location. YPP-234 cannot be moved. The tiniest speck of breach, it gets out. I wanted to incinerate it. That's the only way to destroy it now. It's been sealed in its own cylinder, one that's been changed several times and it still infected other strains in the chamber. Moving it would be a disaster."

Lenore indicted she was going to speak. "What is the delivery system? I mean the transference would be difficult without it escaping, but then again, I lack the knowledge you have."

"That's the beauty of it," replied Brayden. "It doesn't need a bomb, or capsule or powder. The delivery system is one infected human. That was the plan of delivery. For example, one prisoner of war is released and they are infected. For the first twenty-four hours they aren't contagious nor symptomatic. After that, they expel it at a rate that is higher than any R Naught factor we know... And yet, for five days, still no symptoms as they spread the strain. Trust me, the carrier will make it look like Typhoid Mary was passing out daisies. Day seven the carrier gets sick. There are two saving graces to this weapon. The first being that in fifty percent of the cases, the first severe symptoms are shown in the infected after twenty-four hours, some at thirty-six."

"How is that a saving grace?" Lenore asked.

"Because the faster it kills, the less it will spread."

"The other saving grace?"

"There will be people who are naturally resistant to this bacteria."

Morrows questioned, "How do you know this so in depth? Was it tested on animals?"

Brayden shook his head. "No, sir. There was an accident in a lab located in a small village. Fortunately it never escaped the boundaries, and it was eradicated there by severe means."

"A village," said Oren. "Would this be in one of the countries you tried to sell the weapon to?" He held up his hand to Lenore and the others when they vocalized their shock. "Do I need to bring General Scott back in here?"

Brayden shrugged. "You can. I didn't try to sell it. Yes, a Russian scientist had it only because he was trying to help me beat it. He's brilliant. You can look at my documentation. I'm hiding nothing."

Oren nodded. "Let's bring General Scott back in here."

Meeting done.

Lenore exhaled heavily and for the first time in years, she truly wanted a drink. She had a bottle hidden in her office for such an occasion.

"Lenore," said Morrows. "We lost this one. Both were convincing, but General Scott was a bit more convincing."

"Nonsense. Nothing substantiates he was trying to sell this bio-weapon. It's a he said, he said." Lenore walked into her office. "You saw his face. That bio-weapon scares him."

Morrows followed. "What can we do?"

Stopping at a desk, she tapped her finger and smiled. "Take a vacation. A secret vacation. Katie," she turned to her aide seated at the desk. "Once Senator Morrows gets you the number of people going, I need you to make travel arrangements for us to go to Murcia, Spain. Hotel, everything, and it is to be confidential."

"Yes, ma'am," Katie said. "I'll start getting things in order."

"We still have the issue of getting in there," said Morrows.

Lenore smiled. "That's what we have Doctor Brayden for. He worked there, right. I'm sure not everyone is his enemy. Once we are close to travel time, I'll get him to help us. We're finding that bio-weapon," she said. "We're getting in that lab and no one will be the wiser."

THREE – OF KITTENS AND PENS

Baldwin, PA

Ellis Ridge knew he had to get moving, finish packing, and spend some time with his family before he left for the airport. But the thirty-seven year old father was too engrossed in watching the ridiculous hearings on weapons.

They had come to a close and he probably would have to wait until he landed in London to find out anything. He could get lucky and something would be said on his layover, but he doubted it.

His clothes were packed in one suitcase, nice and neat, too. His wife Britney, or Bebe as he called her, made sure of that. She even threw a fabric softener sheet in there. She also put one change of clothes in his carry on, in case his luggage got lost. The meeting was far too important to not have clean clothes.

Ellis was sort of slender, but boasted he had a dad bod. He stood with one arm draped over his waist watching the news on his wife's desktop as if a sports event.

"Come on, tell me something new," he said out loud.

A clunk caught his attention and he spun around. "Bebe? You okay? Did you or one of the kids fall?"

"No, that was the radiator again," she replied, her voice coming from another room. "I'll call the super tomorrow. Can you come in here, lunch is done."

"Yes. Yes." Ellis backed up, stopped, looked once more then

exited out. "Coming. Sorry."

A hallway led from the back two bedrooms of the apartment to the main area which consisted of a living room and eat in kitchen. Hurrying, Ellis tripped up some on the throw rug then nearly sailed across the floor when his foot caught a matchbox car. "Damn it."

He walked through the living room and noticed the television was off. "I thought you were watching the hearings?" he asked as he walked into the small kitchen.

"They ended forty minutes ago," Bebe said.

"They're still discussing them."

"El, they're done for the day. Sit. Come on."

"It's cold in here."

"Again, another reason to call the super."

"Yeah, well be careful with that." Ellis kissed his one-year-old daughter who sat in the high chair, then his five-year-old son, before sitting down. "We're three weeks late on the rent."

"Doesn't matter, we need heat." She placed a plate before him. "Baked sandwich. No cheese. I have broth, too. I know you don't like foods that cause gas when you get on a plane."

"Thank you. Yeah, it's bad enough when you get cramped in, but I don't want to be that guy."

Bebe giggled. "You're funny."

"So what do you think?"

"About?" Bebe joined the table.

Ellis looked at his wife, her dark hair, with long bangs that danced just above her big eyes. "You look really beautiful today."

"Ellis." She waved out her hand.

"You do."

"Thank you. What do I think about what?"

"The hearings."

"They were a waste of time." Bebe said, feeding the youngest a spoonful of applesauce. "I think that doctor guy is so in on everything. I think the reason he turned everyone in is because he is setting up the US for when he sells off that weapon."

"Setting up the US how?" Ellis asked.

"They investigate, go to this Spanish Lab, weapon is gone, because you know, you can't secretly inspect something if you announce you're coming. Sort of like when the super is inspecting the apartment. If he showed up at the door unannounced, hey, the place may be a mess. But he gives us a heads up."

"That's the writer in you talking," Ellis said. "You have that writer brain."

"Thank you. Speaking of writing. I put some pages in your laptop case if you have time to read on the plane."

"I have plenty of time. I am so curious about your new novel."

"Harem Romance, all the rage. I'm giving it a shot." She pointed her fork at him. "You have to be honest with me if it sucks."

"I promise." Ellis didn't lie and he never broke promises, but he wasn't going to tell his wife her writing sucked. Not that it would. She wrote well.

"So," Bebe exhaled the word. "How nervous are you?"

"Very. Super. Every extreme word you can think of."

Actually nervous was an understatement, this was big for him, very big. The meeting would change his life for the better if it went through. Of course, even though he was the brain child he owed it all to James Conroy. Without him, Ellis wouldn't be hours away from getting on a plane.

Ellis had studied, received a degree and failed to get a good paying job in his career of computer science. He never stopped looking, but he had a family and needed to support them and get benefits.

Having worked at McDonalds in high school and most of college, Ellis got a job as a manager in the food industry, Panera Bread to be exact and that was where he met James, a regular.

James dummied down what he did for a living, saying he was a teacher who educated future weather men and women. When Ellis heard that he told James, "Remind me one day to tell you my idea for a program that will revolutionize weather prediction to like ninety percent accuracy."

It was the right person at the right time.

Ellis went to work on the program. He wasn't able to take those extra midnight bakery shifts at other locations, so money became even tighter. It helped some that Bebe's writing was bringing in a few hundred a month.

It would pay off

He hoped.

James set up the meetings with investors and within thirty-six hours they would be presenting their prototype to the Storm Prediction Center at a National Oceanic and Atmospheric Administration conference in London.

"You got this sweetie," Bebe said. "I mean it. You have tested this the whole last year and how many times were you off on the weather. Fifteen?"

"Seventeen."

"It's amazing. You're gonna be calling and telling me you got this."

"Then it will be hanging up the apron, bye-bye Panera Bread." Ellis glanced over to his wife. Her look of pride was genuine. All he wanted to do was give her a great life and he was so close to doing so. The acceptance of the program not only would give him a job, but set them up for life.

His kids could go to college and not have to take on all the debt that Ellis had.

The only bad thing about it all was Ellis would be away for a week. He had never gone that long without seeing his family. But he couldn't let that hang over his head, a week wasn't really that long, he would see them again before he knew it.

FOUR – NARROW ESCAPE

PRESENT DAY
U.S. Army Biological Warfare Laboratories (USBWL)
LAB 27 – 20 miles East, Murcia, Spain

"Why do people do that?" Morrows asked. "It makes no sense."

"I know." Lenore stared out the window of the SUV impatiently wanting to get to the lab. She had received a frantic call from Katie about the attack and Katie hadn't called any police. So Lenore did. But that was fifteen minutes earlier. "Driver, how much longer?"

"Few minutes."

She nodded and sat back, she felt the comfort of Morrows' hand when he reached over and grabbed hers. "Please, Dirk, tell me I didn't lead our people to slaughter."

"This is not your fault. We don't know anything. All we have is the word of a frantic girl who said there was an active shooter."

At that moment any worries about the lab and why they were going went out the window. Lenore was worried about the aides and the workers in the lab. She glanced out the rear window to the SUV, knowing that Oren and Senator Matthews were feeling the dread as well.

When they pulled up they were first stopped by police who let them through and that was when Lenore saw not only a large police presence, but military vans and ambulances.

No sooner had she seen the bullet riddled SUV's parked out front, Lenore saw Katie seated in the back of an ambulance with a blanket around her shoulders speaking to a police officer.

The moment the SUV parked, Lenore rushed out and ran to Katie. She threw her arms around the woman, nearly hyperventilating.

"I'm sorry. I'm so sorry you went through this," Lenore said.

"I'm okay, I'll be okay," Katie sobbed. "I didn't see who did it. I just heard the shots and ran."

Lenore placed her hand on Katie's face. "You made it out. That's what's important."

The office, who spoke English nodded at the ambulance driver then turned to Lenore. "We believe she is in shock. They are taking her to have her looked at soon. We'll question her some more later."

"Yes. Thank you." Lenore nodded and peered back into the ambulance. "Katie, don't you worry. As soon as I can I am getting you back to New York. Okay?"

"Thank you." Katie sobbed.

"I'll find you at the hospital or hotel, I have to first speak to Senator Morrows," Lenore said, and then finally turned around to take it all in. It was too much and heartbreaking.

Seeing the other senators talking to authorities, Lenore noticed Morrows speaking to a frazzled man in a suit. When Morrows saw her, he walked from the man to Lenore.

"Hey," Lenore said. "Anything?"

Morrows looked over his shoulder, then scratched his head. "Everyone is dead."

Lenore gasped, her hand shooting to her mouth. "Oh my God."

"Do we know why the military is here?"

"Because of the BSL4 lab below and they were the fastest team they could get in there to check on things. Come on, I'll introduce you to the director." He took Lenore by the arm and led her to the older gentlemen. "Bill Latone, this is Senator Lenore

James."

Lenore was taken aback. "You're American."

"I am. Sorry to meet under these circumstances," he said with a shake of her hand. "I arrived a few minutes before the police and found the young woman from your team inside one of the SUVs. She wasn't in the car when it happened. She was on the pre-tour with the early group. They would have been on the first floor when it all transpired."

"There are no survivors?"

"We don't know what's going on below. Spain's Valencia team is getting ready to go to the BSL4 lab. The good news is the elevator is still locked and the stairwell is engaged. Both are controlled by biometrics. So we are hopeful there are survivors down there."

"Do we know who did this?" Lenore asked.

Bill shook his head. "Not yet. We'll review security footage at our offsite facility. Just... the strange thing is we have alarms. Silent panic alarms as well. The offsite facility received nothing. They think they were disabled."

"An inside job?" asked Lenore.

"Possibly. Maybe a former employee."

"Could they have gotten below?"

"Yes and that's a frightening prospect if bullets are flying around down there."

"Bill,' Morrows said. "You know why we're here. You have got to be straight with us. Is this a US Military lab?"

"It's a difficult question to answer. It's not yes or no," Bill replied. "It is not a US Military lab. However, they use it. They have a lab down there."

Another gasp escaped Lenore and her insides trembled some. "Is there a YPP-234 here?"

"I cannot confirm or deny that," said Bill. "They don't tell me what they have, but I know they have something dangerous that they had special robotics to work on it and won't be in the same room even with PPE equipment. And that's what worries me. One bullet hole, I shudder to think."

"Jesus it is there," Lenore said in a quiet shock.

Morrows inhaled then exhaled loudly as he spoke. "When the Valencia team goes down. We'll know soon enough. Hopefully nothing got out."

Got out. Lenore slowly turned around and saw them placing Katie in the ambulance. Muttering an 'excuse me', she rushed over before they left. "Can I just ..." she lifted a hand to the EMT worker closing the door. "Speak to her real fast."

He nodded and paused.

"Katie, I'm sorry to bother you. It was here, Katie."

"What?" Katie asked confused.

"The reason we came."

Katie's eyes widened. "Oh no."

Lenore nodded. "Yes. We don't know if there was a breach with it. I just have to ask and I know the chances are slim to none, but... you weren't below in the BSL4 level were you."

Katie hesitated before answering. "No."

Oh," Lenore sighed in relief. "Thank God. Now, go. Get checked out."

Stepping back, Lenore gave a compassionate smile to Katie, keeping her eyes on her until they closed the ambulance doors.

She was relieved that not only did Katie get out, she wasn't on that particular lab floor. Now Lenore just had to hope that Katie wasn't the only thing that got out.

FIVE – SHORT LIVED MYSTERY

Mt. Lebanon, PA

Josh.

Send.

Josh.

Send.

In her frustration, Jennifer Brayden had resorted to one word texts to her husband Josh.

Prior to that, she was sending him texts, social media messages and calling constantly. Only on this day she had heard nothing.

Nothing for twenty-four hours.

Each time she called and left a voice message, she would get a reply in the form of text saying simply, 'I'm alright. Be home soon."

The last she saw him was when he left for Washington D.C. to testify at the hearing, after that they spoke on the phone.

Josh assured her everything was going to be fine and he had to take care of some things.

Jennifer was genuinely worried about him. Not that he didn't seem fine when she spoke to him, but he was officially a whistleblower.

Was he in danger?

After two days of speaking on the phone briefly, their exchanges went directly to text messages then finally, it was no longer conversations it was just responses.

When he went to the hearing six days earlier, their lawyer told them to expect a media frenzy, but it didn't happen. She went to work every day at the elementary school where she returned to teaching just a year before. She had taken a leave of absence for good reasons.

The weekend had come and gone, it was Tuesday and every chance she had she tried to contact him. His recent behavior wasn't like him.

She went to the store, the coffee shop, and each time sat in her car just trying to reach him.

The hearings didn't go as expected. Why did no one believe Josh?

She did.

Of course, she did. He told her about YPP-234 a couple years prior.

It was his brainchild and his escape.

She had known Josh since the seventh grade and they were in youth group at the church. He was always ambitious and smart. She married him before he started working for the government and followed him everywhere.

Together twenty-six years, married twenty-two, he told her everything. Then when they lost their only son, nineteen, to an overdose, everything changed.

That was four years ago, and about the same time YPP-234 came about.

Jennifer quit teaching and after a year moved back to her roots to be near her family and Josh traveled for his job.

They saw each other, loved each other, but things had changed.

They hadn't recovered from their loss.

How could anyone? They just, like so many parents who had been through the same, learned to live with it.

But both of them had this underlying feeling of not fearing death or if they lived or died. A part of Jennifer always wondered if that was how YPP-234 came about.

Despite the physical distance, they were close and friends, which played into why she worried so much.

She tried calling the Senator's office, colleagues that knew Josh. Nothing. No news.

As a last resort she would call the police and file a missing person's report. For that she'd give it one more day. In her gut, she felt he was alive and fine, after all his phone was off, the messages went through. But his location sharing wasn't on. Something was different. Amiss.

Where was her husband?

<><><><>

All Doctor Josh Brayden could think about was Jen. He had never gone an entire day without talking to her and he knew she had to be worried. There was nothing he could do. They took his phone a day earlier. After being moved for days on end by car from hotel to hotel, Josh was then non-stop. He had been traveling for twenty-four hours, one plane to the next. Each plane was private, shades drawn and he wasn't permitted to look out.

When he was removed from the plane and transferred to the next plane he was blindfolded.

Finally, after the fourth flight, he wasn't placed on another plane. He was put into a van, his blindfold removed once he was securely inside.

It was warm where he was, a bit muggy. They drove for a little while, not long, and he knew they arrived when they covered his eyes once more and took him inside somewhere.

The temperature changed to a cool, crisp air conditioned room, he could hear the ocean, smell it. He also smelled coffee and food.

When the blindfold was removed, he was in front of a table with a bountiful feast, coffee and juice.

"Sit please," the male voice instructed.

Josh looked behind him and saw the man. He knew instantly who it was. He had spoken to him, knew him only as A, but had never met him.

A fit man in an undecorated military uniform. No name, no markings. He was around fifty and didn't look shady. Well put together and refined was more like it. A distinguished man with gray hair. Josh would have bet money he could have been a high stakes European fashion model in his day.

'A' joined him at the table, finally giving his first name as he sat, "Alek, call me Alek. Please eat. I know you must be hungry."

"I am," Josh replied. "But I am also worried about my wife. I haven't spoken to her and it's out of character."

"Soon. I apologize for the traveling," he said. "And taking your phone. We cannot chance you being followed or traced."

"I understand." Josh took a sip of his coffee, it was probably the best he ever had.

"Thank you, Doctor."

Josh gazed up. "I will assume since this was the big travel day …"

"It's the end of our relationship yes. You will be returned to a location you know, but being a married man myself, I will give you the ability to contact your wife after we're through."

"So it's done?" Josh asked.

Alek nodded. "Yes. It is done. It was a success, all information you gave worked out beautifully."

"You got it?" he asked.

Again, Alek nodded. "We did."

"And your people took extreme caution?"

"Just like you instructed, and we rehearsed it many times. It was perfect, they will see very little on the cameras. Again, I cannot thank you enough."

"Well …" Josh chuckled.

Alek smiled. "As we speak, the money is being transferred. It will not be traceable." An envelope sat next to Alek's plate and he pushed it forward to Josh. "Instructions on how to obtain the money without attention."

"Thank you."

"Now that our business has successfully concluded, shall we feast?" Alex lifted his hands.

"Yes. It's looks fantastic," Josh said. "Let's eat."

Josh helped himself to everything on that table and did so happily. He didn't feel guilt or remorse for what he had done, he was optimistic and positive.

It all went as planned, from the whistleblowing to the hearings.

But now it was done, Josh was a very rich man. He planned to get Jen and take her wherever she wanted to go, live far away, heal from the pain, and be together. A fresh start after his son Matt's death.

It was more than a new beginning.

It was a breach of trust, breach of ethnics, but more so, unknowingly, a breach in the lab that had just unleashed the world's deadliest weapon.

PART TWO

CONFIDENTIAL CONTROL

SIX – SCREEN CUES

London, England

The room service tray set on the small table of Ellis' hotel room. The food he ordered was barely touched. Not because it wasn't any good, it was, but his appetite wasn't there. Every time he thought about food, he got a knot in his stomach.

He really thought he would have heard a decision from the conference. Maybe it didn't work that way. Probably not. Everything went well. He was fearful when the days rolled by and they hadn't even been called.

What if they blew them off? Ellis had maxed out his credit card for the airfare and the hotel took what money he had put away for the new tires on their car.

He gambled.

It was strange, he imagined it like a sales pitch. James would get up there and 'sell' it, but it was as if they were featured speakers.

The panel of scientists applauded with enthusiasm and cheers. People approached them and said how blown away they were.

Yet, no one said. "We want to buy that software."

It was pushing check out time, then off to the airport to fly home. Ellis felt deflated even though there was no reason to. He just wanted to leave London on a high note.

He kept reminding himself no news was good news.

More than anything he wanted to bring good news to his wife. But the last he spoke with her, all he could say was the truth which was, he was still waiting.

He took another bite of his toast and swig of his coffee, then walked over and closed his suitcase.

After checking the time, he gathered his charger, and the chips he bought the night before and placed them in his carryon bag. As he readied that, a knock came at his door.

It had to be James hurrying him along and Ellis walked over to open it.

"Hey," Ellis said as he opened the door and saw James. "Just finishing up." He turned to walk away and he noticed James just standing there. "Dude, you can come in."

James didn't.

"You alright?" Ellis asked.

Slowly, almost as if he practiced it, James grinned.

"What?" Ellis asked cautiously.

"Next Monday, we go to DC and sign those papers."

"We got it?"

"We got it," James said coolly then drew in his clenched fist.

Ellis wasn't as calm.

"Oh my God!" Ellis shrieked, jumped out of the doorframe and grabbed on to James with an excited embrace. "Oh my God!'

James laughed.

Slam.

His room door closed and locked.

"Shit," Ellis said.

"Your key is in there huh?"

Ellis nodded. "Eh, I'll go to the front desk. It's fine. You know why? Nothing will dampen this day or ruin it."

<><><><>

Murcia, Spain

It was insanity at its best, Lenore wanted to scream in frustration, but there was nothing she could do but wait, and she did, then Bill Latone called her to meet in the afternoon, he had encouraging news.

Senator Morrows had left with Katie at dawn, he needed to personally speak to the family of his aide.

"I'm on my way," Lenore spoke on the phone. "We're meeting at his offsite security building. What time is your flight to New York?"

Katie replied, "I'm on the one forty-five, Senator Morrows' flight left a couple hours ago."

"Oh my, you've been there a while."

"Yeah, but I'm relaxing in the lounge. I'll be on the plane soon."

"Contact me when you land, okay?"

"Will do."

"Safe travels." Lenore ended the call. She was grateful Katie was okay. She was lucky, making it out of there when no one else did.

Now that Katie was situated and on her way home, Lenore focused on the task at hand.

Bill was hopeful for answers.

Finally.

Twenty-four hours had passed since the attack.

The police were involved, Spain's version of the FBI, the military. The news of the massacre hadn't broken, but it would. Although they'd leave out the information about it being a BSL4 lab.

Lenore just needed to know. Did the weapon get out?

Because of YPP-234 they hadn't gone down to the labs, not even the military. They were going to, but Bill stopped them.

It wasn't stable and until they knew, they had to wait, just on the outside chance it was breached.

There was no response or answer from anyone who worked down below, so chances were they were hit as well.

The questions remained; did they get the biological agent, did one stray bullet pierce the chamber?

When her SUV pulled up to the building, Bill was outside waiting on her.

"Tell me you know something," Lenore said.

"We're almost there. Come on in." He opened the door for her.

"What are we looking for?" she asked, slowing down when she saw a lot of people there.

There were two men in suits that immediately looked at her when she stepped in, in fact they made their way to her.

One was older maybe near retirement, the other younger.

"Senator James?" the older man spoke, showing his badge.

It was FBI, but it was different. Lenore recognized it right away. He was a legal attaché. A special agent that worked internationally on cases under the authority, and with the government, that contacted them. Spain wasted no time, and that made Lenore feel better.

"I'm special agent Danvers," the older agent said. "And this is Agent Small. We've been briefed on the situation. Right now we have our best computer people working on the cameras and we're hoping to get some answers soon."

With a puzzled look, Lenore turned to Bill. "So there was a reason we hadn't watched the footage."

Bill nodded. "Someone hacked into the lines, blocking them. Hopefully they didn't erase them."

Lenore ran her hand over her face. "So without a doubt, this was an inside job,"

Agent Danvers replied, "We think so. Someone overrode the system. Hijacked the cameras, and if they did make it downstairs, which we believe they did, then someone helped them."

"But we have no one unaccounted for," said Bill. "Okay, let me take that back. Everyone on the main floor is accounted for. The fourteen downstairs, we don't know yet. We can only assume."

"If one of them isn't there," said Danvers, "That may be the one."

"Agent Danvers," a voice called to him.

Danvers lifted his head to a young man standing across the room to acknowledge him.

"We're in," the man said.

<><><><>

Admittedly, Ted Danvers didn't know as much about the case as he hoped, then again, not even Spanish Intelligence knew much. It appeared that the special lab was holding things back. All that was moot, the footage would give him insight into who or what occurred. His years of experience would be helpful in determining if it indeed was an inside job, he felt it was.

Even though access to the feed was being shared with the agency and Spanish intelligence, Danvers was the main investigator on the case. It was all eyes on the footage, not just Danvers'. But he was watching closely.

There were things he needed to do when reviewing the footage. He needed to get the time frame, the shooter or shooters, how long it went on and did they breach the lower lab with everything deadly in the world and then some.

His knowledge of bio-equipment would keep him from one hundred percent determining if that secret weapon was touched, for that he'd call the director, Bill.

But until he gave it a quick review, he needed to know what was on there, so he could warn the Senator and Bill. After all, more than the Senator, Bill had a connection to those in the building. It was going to be hard to watch.

His computer guy, Al, sat before the monitor, next to him was Agent Small, as Danvers stood behind and watched.

"Look," Al pointed to the screen. "You don't even see a car pull up, they walked."

Danvers, one arm crossed over his waist rubbed his chin, while watching. "Is that eight of them?"

"Yes." Al nodded. "Can't get a face. Covered in gas masks."

"Now is that because they want to hide their identity or because of the weapon?" Danvers asked.

"We may still be able to get their identity," Al said. "There's a guy in the Legats office on this now, he has this program that scans features that are visible even with the mask. Plus, eight people, one of them made a mistake somewhere."

"Let's hope," Small spoke up, "And let's hope it's only to hide the identity. But they obviously go downstairs. We haven't heard from anyone in the BSL4 lab. Question is, did they take something or was this an accident?"

"My gut is telling me they went down there for something," Danvers said.

"YPP-234?" asked Small.

"Absolutely. It's not smallpox or Ebola, they can get that at any BSL4 lab. They came here for something specific."

"Then we need more than the vague notes of Doctor Brayden," said Small. "We need to find out more about this thing and what would happen if it got out."

"If it got out," replied Danvers. "It's not gonna matter what we know."

Slowly releasing a deep breath, Danvers watched the footage. It was methodical, not radical or random. The eight person kill team knew exactly what they were doing.

Those in the atrium didn't stand a chance or get a second to flee and hide.

"They had the layout," said Small. "Everything. They knew."

Danvers nodded, watching as they went down halls, dividing up in teams of two. "I want the footage to see if they went below."

The screen on the monitor switched to multiple views and Al pulled up the footage of the hallway with the elevator and staircase.

"Ah man," Al sighed out, sitting back. "Those two women thought they were safe."

"I would," stated Danvers. "It's a biometric system. Why would they think they could be followed?"

One of the two gunmen in pursuit of the woman held his hand to the biometric reader by the staircase. He did so as if he had done it before a hundred times, no hesitation.

"Stop," Danvers instructed. "Go back to when the woman opened the elevator."

"Yes, sir." Al rewound slowly.

Danvers didn't blink, he didn't want to miss it. "Stop when it lights up."

"Got it."

The woman's hand raised to the control and the second it lit green, Al stopped it on the frame,

"There." Danvers pointed. "Zoom in."

Al did.

"See it has her name. Go to the shooter opening the stairwell," Danvers instructed.

"How is that possible?" asked Small. "It goes by your hand, right? He's wearing a glove."

Al shook his head. "This was planned for a while so they found the tech for it to work. Here." He stopped the footage then zoomed in.

There was no name. Just four 'ones' where the name should have been.

"What the hell?" Danvers asked.

"Defiantly hacked that, too," said Al.

"Keep going."

They stayed on the two shooters in the stairwell rather than those who were on the main floor. They didn't walk down the four flights of stairs, they nearly ran in synch, making it below in no time.

Once on that level, they split up, with one of them looking exactly like he knew where he was going. Danvers picked that camera view to watch. That one single shooter, with the build of a man, made his way down a short series of hall, using his gloved hand to open every secure door, and taking out anyone in his way, until he arrived.

But there was a problem Danvers could see and it was one mentioned by the director, Bill. There were two technicians or scientists, whatever they were, in that room, not only wearing PPE, but using robotic arms to work on something on the other side of a glass window. When the shooter fired four times, at some point, it struck that glass window. While it didn't shatter, clearly it was damaged.

That was more of a concern for Danvers than he wanted to admit, but before he went overboard, figuring out what they were going to do, he summoned Bill to watch.

SEVEN – HOMEWARD BOUND

Heathrow Airport, London

When Ellis heard the boarding call for his row, he pulled the charger from the outlet and wrapped it up to place back in his carry on.

"You know." James stood. "It's counterproductive to use the phone while it's charging."

"I know. I know." Ellis shouldered his bag and stood as well. "I wanted to call Bebe with the news."

James glanced at his watch. "It's ten after eight back home. Did you wake her?"

"No," Ellis dragged out the word. "Not at all."

"Oh, that's right. Your oldest has school."

Ellis shook his head. "Deke comes today, so he'll be there when I get home. Beside he's fourteen. He gets himself up for school. But ... the baby gets Bebe up, I just wanted to have her be fully awake when I told her."

"How'd she react?"

"Ecstatic. But I think it will sink in once I get home."

"Did you call Deke?"

"Nah, I'll see him tonight. I'll tell him in person."

The two of them finally joined the line that had backed up.

"Packed flight," said James.

"It is. I downloaded a few movies to watch. Plus the entire Season Five of Blissful Battle Chefs."

"Good show."

"I know, right." Ellis felt the poke to his shoulder.

"Excuse me," a female voice spoke.

Ellis turned around to the young woman behind him. "Yes?"

"Did they board first class yet?" she asked.

Ellis chuckled. "Lady, they boarded that a while ago."

"Oh, shoot."

James looked behind him and inched back. "Be my guest to go ahead of me."

"That is so sweet, thank you." She got in line. "I appreciate it."

"No problem. I never got that," James said.

"What?" asked Ellis?

"Why do they board first class first?" James asked. "I mean, these people pay some bucks for their seats only to have to sit there and watch everyone board."

"Two reasons," Ellis held up his fingers. "Free unlimited drinks and preflight drinks and they can see the shady people first."

The woman they let in the line laughed and turned around. "My boss said that. She used to tell me when flying first class it is our job to keep an eye out for suspicious people."

"Do you?" James asked.

"No. I just want the free drinks."

Both Ellis and James laughed. Not that she was all that funny, but they were being charming. James even helped her get her bag in the overhead compartment before she sat down in 4A.

James claimed he did it to be nice, Ellis knew it was because she was holding up the line.

They made their way through the crowded first class to the empty rows of the main cabin and more so to the rear of the plane where their seats were located.

James had the window seat.

Ellis didn't mind. He liked the aisle seat, it gave him more leg room and he felt less claustrophobic. It truly was going to be a crowded flight, Ellis could see the river of people pouring through.

It didn't matter, they would be in the air soon and Ellis would be deep into his tablet watching shows to pass time until he got home. His lay over at JFK was short and within eleven hours he'd be home. It seemed like a long time, but it really wasn't. In less than a day, he'd be back with his family with a bright, prosperous future waiting for his family.

<><><><>

Bill Latone sat with Lenore in that room, asking Danvers, "How disturbing is this going to be? Do I want to see this?"

"No," Danvers replied. "But I need you to see this. We're only going to show you just a small segment. There is damage to a glass window in a lab the gunman entered. We need you to identify if that is the lab where this YPP is kept. Okay?"

Bill nodded and only needed to watch three seconds of the video. The shooter hadn't even taken a life, when Bill spoke up. 'Yes. That's the lab."

"You're sure?" Danvers asked.

"Positive."

Lenore spoke softly. "He knew exactly where to go."

"Oh, yeah." Danvers nodded. "He knew codes, knew where the transport cases were."

"So he got it?" Lenore asked.

"He got something," Danvers replied. "Al, go to the cameras in that contained room."

"Wait." Bill said. "You don't need the 'in room' cameras, the camera on the robotic arm will give you exact details what specimen he took. You can tap into one of those."

Danvers shook his head. "No. He didn't use that."

"He went in?" Bill asked with panic. "Dear God, I don't know this weapon, but I do know it isn't stable and that is why robotics were used. That glass window is the least of your worries."

"But we haven't determined if he got it," said Lenore. "We haven't seen what he took."

Bill shook his head. "Doesn't matter. All last night I was

reviewing the information you have me from Doctor Brayden. That weapon is a beast."

"Maybe now is the time we get a hold of Doctor Brayden," said Lenore. "I'll get my people on it. He designed it, he knows it."

Agent Small indicated to another screen. "The doors sealed when they both left that floor. Would that help?"

Bill nodded. "It could. I don't know, but I do know, if this weapon is as bad as those reports from Brayden state, we need to find these people who took it. Let's hope the man who grabbed it was protected somehow."

"If he was," Danvers said. "Those doors sealed and everyone died tragically, so if that weapon was in the air down there. It stayed down there." His phone rang. "Can you excuse me?" He stepped back and took the brief call. When it ended, he rushed over to the computer. "Al, I need you to go to seventeen minutes, three seconds after the terrorists leave. There's a survivor."

"Of course, there is," Lenore said. "Katie, my aide, she survived. She hid in the atrium."

The screen before Al was filled with different camera angles. His eyes shifting to each one as his hands worked. "There. I got her." Al backed up the footage. "Is that her?" He paused the footage.

"Yes," Lenore answered. "That's her."

"Oh my God," Bill gasped. "Is she leaving the BSL4 floor? She is." He moved closer to the screen. "If that weapon escaped, it escaped with her. She was down there seventeen minutes."

"Senator," Danvers said. "We need to find her. Where is she?"

Lenore glanced at Danvers with an expression that screamed no less than sheer horror. She shook her head. "It's not good."

<><><><>

"Ladies and Gentlemen we have reached cruising altitude, you can feel free to move about the cabin, I hope you enjoy your flight."

Katie raised her eyes to the speaker above her head where the pilot's voice came from. She had no intention of moving about the cabin. She lifted a hand to signal the flight attendant for a drink.

Once the attendant's attention was caught, she made her way to Katie.

"Please, a white wine."

"Absolutely." The flight attendant acknowledged the request with a smile.

Katie thanked her and then thought about logging into the Wi-Fi system, checking her email or social media. But she had time for that. She wanted to relax, the night before she got back to the hotel late after all the questioning and check up at the hospital. A drink, a nap, then maybe the tablet.

It was a long flight, but she was happy she was going home.

EIGHT – TRACING THE PATH

It was a weapon.

Though biologically based on one of the oldest known pathogens, it was still a weapon.

Twenty-four hours after exposure, the weapon is activated. What made YPP-234 powerful and deadly was that each new infection created another weapon.

A communicability rate so high, none other had even measured in the range. Not even measles which held the highest known contagion.

YPP-234 buried Measles.

Fortunately for the workers and guests at Starbucks, the internal, silent weapon in Katie hadn't activated until she arrived at the front desk. Of the four people behind her, two became the next weapon.

One from Spain, the other from Italy.

The front desk clerk was spared.

However, Senator Morrows was not. She not only shared a cab with him, she shared the weapon in her. The plastic window protected the cab driver.

Senator Morrows would go on to visit his aide's family then attend a fundraiser function in Texas.

At the airport, Katie passed it on to the skycap and the security agent. Both of which, in twenty-four hours would share their new found, death causing ability to half of the thousands that they came in contact with.

She and Senator Morrows enjoyed a drink at the bar where the bartender got a kind of tip he didn't want. She met a charming and handsome Russian model, he took the weapon home.

A flight, another airport, and another flight.

Katie's mother always taught her to share, but she didn't mean a deadly weapon.

While Katie wasn't the only one spreading the weapon after the initial breach, the gunman that took the weapon from the containment was the other.

Both of their actions would cause a ripple effect that was unstoppable.

They just didn't know it yet.

NINE – CALL FOR HELP

Mt. Lebanon, PA

.

Ignorance was bliss and as long as Josh claimed ignorance, he was happy. He didn't want to know how they got YPP-234 or what measures they took to obtain it, it wasn't his problem.

He made a deal, how they handled it was their doing.

The only details he wanted to know was how he was going to get the money without drawing suspicion.

Simply a faux research lab was set up, the money was in there and Josh would receive a weekly paycheck as if he worked for them.

Before he even got out of bed, he checked the balance of his bank account and smiled.

The first installment was in there.

He arrived back home so late the night before, Jen was in bed, he didn't want to disturb her so he slept in Matthew's room. That was really nothing new. He slept in his son's room a lot. Whenever he really was missing Matt, or when something triggered instant, intense heartbreak he crawled into his son's bed.

Certain that Jen had left for work, Josh jumped in the shower and was surprised when he emerged to the smell of food cooking.

He got dressed, went downstairs and straight to the kitchen.

"Hey, babe," he said, walking up to Jen and kissing her on the cheek. 'Are you sick? Why are you home?'

"I took a personal day, since you came home and never said a word."

"I didn't want to wake you."

"Josh." Jen said with a hint of desperation. "Is there someone else?"

"What? Oh my God, no. No." He shook his head. "I just ... I've been trying to negotiate a contract with a new company. This hearing thing put a damper on it, a lot of questions."

"Did it work out?" she asked.

"I think it did. When I went back for my phone, which by the way was still on the charger in the corner of the reception area, I spoke to them. It looks good. In fact, it looks great. Maybe you know, maybe we can move there."

"You didn't say where 'there' was," Jen said.

"Switzerland."

"Oh, Josh, another country? I don't know if I can be that far away from all that reminds me of Matt."

"Maybe that's what we need."

Jen seemed hesitant to ever react. She handed Josh a cup of coffee and in the middle of the exchange, the doorbell rang.

"I'll get it," Josh said, taking his coffee.

"Are you sure."

"Positive. You're cooking." He thanked her and sipped his coffee as he made his way to the front door and opened it.

Two men in suits stood there.

"Doctor Joshua Brayden?" the one asked.

"Yes."

The man showed his badge. "FBI."

Internally, Josh trembled a bit. "Something ... something wrong."

"Senator James has been trying to reach you," he said.

"My phone has been off. What's going on?"

The other agent pulled out a tablet and after swiping a few times, Lenore's voice came out.

"Did you find him?" she asked.

"Right here, Ma'am." The agent handed Josh the tablet.

"Come in," Josh said, stepping away from the door and into the foyer with the tablet. "Senator, this must be important if you're tracking me down." He was prepared to be questioned by her about the weapon, he wasn't prepared for what she was about to tell him.

"We need your help, STAT," she said. "YPP-234, is in the wild."

TEN – LAST FLIGHT

Baldwin, PA

Bebe made airplane noises as she moved the spoon of smashed peas to Baby Ginny's mouth, it was silly to do, but Ginny loved it. Everyone once and a while Bebe would pause to really listen to the podcast playing on her tablet. It was one of the shows Ellis hated that she listened to. The Pierson Wayne, Piercing Truth show. One of those guys who found a conspiracy in everything. Not that Bebe believed them, but she found them entertaining.

Something caught her attention, her hand hovered just before delivering the spoon to Ginny.

The baby wasn't happy about that, the little girl kept trying to get her food but Bebe kept moving back.

The podcaster mentioned a mass shooting at a cosmetics lab in Murcia Spain, something about a disgruntled employee. But it wasn't the tragic mass shooting that drew her attention it was the city.

"Oh, sorry," she said to Ginny and gave her the spoon. "Mommy is trying to figure out why that city sounds so familiar."

Ginny moved her mouth for more.

"Not like Mommy is a geography person. But I know that name." She fed the baby then looked to the stove for the time. She thought about using Messenger to send a message to Ellis to ask him, but realized he only paid for Wi-Fi for four hours and that was up ten minutes earlier. She guessed she could wait. He would be landing in New York soon enough.

In the middle of another bite of food delivery to the baby,

Bebe heard the lock to the front door of the apartment being disengaged. The door opened and closed. She worried because no one was supposed to be walking in. She stood from the chair.

"Hello?" she called out.

"It's me Bebe," the younger male voice called out.

Bebe exhaled. "Deke, you scared me. Why aren't you in school?"

"I had an early dismissal. Doctor's appointment," he said as he walked into the kitchen.

Her nearly fifteen year old stepson was tall, he would for sure be taller than Ellis. In fact, he looked like a younger version.

"Hey." Deke kissed Bebe on the cheek and then the baby. "How's my Ginny. Gin, Gin." He spoke in a higher pitch voice.

Ginny smiled.

"Any word from Dad?" Deke asked as he sat down.

"He'll be landing soon in New York."

"Yeah, but ... any word?" Deke asked. "Did he or did he not get it?"

"I'll let him explain it all."

Deke grinned. "I bet its good news."

"You want something to eat."

"Nah, Mom got me McDonald's. I'm good." He turned his focus to the baby and took the spoon from Bebe to take over feeding duty...

"Hey, Deke, does the city Murcia, Spain sound familiar. It sounds familiar to me, why is that?"

"Because of those hearings you and dad were watching."

Exhaling and sitting back with an 'Oh', Bebe nodded. "That's right, thank you."

"Why?"

"Get this. There was a shooting at a cosmetics lab there. Strange huh? Wouldn't think Murcia would be a lab capital. Pittsburgh maybe."

"Maybe it's not a cosmetic lab. Maybe it's that bio lab and they're trying to cover it up. Dude, how sick would that be?"

"Okay now you're sounding like Pierson Wayne." Shaking

her head with a smile, Bebe stood. She didn't want to tell Deke his joking theory was actually pretty good, and without Deke seeing, Bebe logged into the chatroom of the Pierson Wayne show and tossed that theory out there. Of course there were so many people logged in, no one would probably see it.

<><><><>

Mr. Lebanon, Pa

"Josh, Josh, what are you doing?" Jen asked him, sounding almost panicked as she followed him around and into the garage.

"We don't have time, Jen." He stood in the back of the garage. "Where is it? Yes, here it is." He grabbed a large gray Rubbermaid bin.

"Does this frantic attitude have anything to do with the FBI that was here?"

He turned around. "More than you think."

"I know you took that call, but you didn't say anything other than you have to go to Washington D.C."

"I do. I didn't say anything for a good reason, I needed to know more. I will explain it in the car." Josh took off the lid and dumped the contents on the floor.

"In the ... uh!" she shrieked. "That's the Christmas stuff."

"I don't care. It's now the food bin." He walked by her. "I need another. I'll come back for it after I get this one done. I need you to pack clothes. Clothes and blankets. You name it."

"Josh, this is insane."

"I know." He walked fast and to the kitchen. "Get moving, Jen. Pack. Pack for a while."

"I'm not going to D.C."

"No, you're not. I am." He began to just empty things from the walk in the pantry into the bin.

"Josh, if we need to get food, we can stop at the store."

He paused. "No, we cannot." He then muttered as he looked over items. "I'm only putting nonperishable in here. Watch the expiration dates. Where's the cooler? We're taking the meat from the freezer."

"Oh my God, Josh, stop." She held up her hand.

"Put the cold stuff away as soon as you get there."

"Where am I going?"

He ignored her. "Freezer bags."

"Right behind you. Josh."

"Break up the meat when you get there." He held the box of freezer bags. "Make it last. Batteries."

"Behind you as well."

"Thanks. Jen, why are you standing there? Go pack."

"If I am not going to D.C., where am I going? I can't just go."

"Yes, you will," Josh said.

"Are you in trouble with those FBI guys? Are we running?"

"We're running, but not from the FBI. Or rather, you're running."

"Where am I going?" she asked. "Please tell me."

"I'm taking a detour on my way to D.C. I am taking you somewhere tucked away. Tucked away from everyone. Isolated. You need to be away from everyone."

"For how long?"

"Six weeks."

Jen gasped loudly in disbelief. "I am not going to hide somewhere for six weeks. Tell me what is going on."

"In the car."

"No, you'll tell me now," she demanded. "Right now or I won't do anything. Why am I being tucked away for six weeks?"

"Because it's out."

"What?" she questioned confused.

"Jen, YPP-234 is out. And if we can't stop it, by my calculations," Josh said. "Six weeks is all it's gonna take for the world to be over."

<><><><>

Lenore closed her tablet, leaving it on her tray table. She

glanced up to the flight attendant with a thank-you and accepted the tea.

If she were a drinker, she would be having something hardcore, but all alcohol went to her head immediately and Lenore needed to keep her wits about her.

She was already behind the eight ball. Katie had left Spain and was already on her connecting flight from London to New York by the time Lenore was able to secure a flight. Originally, she had no plans to leave. She wanted to stay behind for the crisis, but when she learned that the crisis was on its way to America, she had to get there.

"I'd say shoot it down," Doctor Brayden had told her on that video call. *"But she isn't the only source. By what you have told me, whoever took it probably is now a weapon as well."*

"It looks that way. But, shoot it down? That's extreme."

"Yes. Extreme is needed. Assuming there are over two hundred people on that flight, that is at least a hundred weapons unleashed in twenty-four hours. What I need to do is create a tracing chart. Get her cell phone records, find out where she was, and trace."

"Is that possible."

"Yes, it's possible. Can we stop it? That ... I'm not sure of."

Lenore was heartbroken. Was it all her fault? She was torturing herself for making Katie leave and go home.

There was no reason to even suspect Katie was lying to her. Lenore believed Katie was in a state of shock and actually didn't remember. She had to be, there was no way the young woman would deny being down in a BSL4 lab knowing there was a possible breach.

Fortunately, Senator Morrows was to land a couple hours ahead of Katie. If Doctor Brayden was correct, Morrows hadn't hit the twenty-four hour mark yet and a five day isolation would contain him.

Doctor Brayden would work closely with the CDC and Bioweapons officials from Fort Detrick. The news would break about the leak soon, and Lenore had to have her story ready.

The world knew about the attack in Murcia, but the press

was told it was a cosmetics lab and nothing deadly.

That couldn't be further from the truth. Lenore just hoped when the truth came out, things were under control and that all started with controlling the flight Katie was on.

<><><><>

"Ladies and Gentlemen," the pilot spoke over the speaker. "We're making our approach to JFK international airport, we'll be on the ground shortly. On behalf of myself and the crew, it has been a pleasure serving you. Thank you for flying US Airlines. We hope you had an enjoyable flight."

Ellis was ready to land and get off the plane. He actually did have an enjoyable flight. He wanted to see New York as they arrived, but James had the shade down and was sleeping.

"Hey, dude," Ellis nudged him. "We're landing."

James grunted.

Ellis looked over to the woman in the seat across the aisle as the plane descended and finally touched down. An older woman, not that old though. Maybe in her sixties. She had a smooth face, not wrinkles, but the young woman with her kept calling her grandma, and that young lady was at least old enough to drink, because she had several.

Two hours into their flight, Ellis learned the woman's name was Ossandra. Or Ossie as everyone called her. They chatted quite a bit. A slightly fluffy but strong woman, whose build inhibited her from reaching for the bag she shoved under the seat in front of her Ellis' first encounter with her was when she pulled out that bag and a slight bump of turbulence caused her rear end to hit Ellis in the arm.

She apologized and Ellis laughed. "It's fine."

Ossie fed him snacks on the plane. Ones she had made. They looked like wagon wheels but reminded him of pork rinds. She had taken her three grandchildren to visit family in Spain. A vacation that took her three years to save for along with a cash prize from a cooking contest.

Ellis didn't mind talking to her. The flight flew by because of her and they probably both knew each other better than they expected to.

Heck, while he still had Wi-Fi he added her on social media.

"You'd get along great with my wife," he told her.

Chances of the two families ever getting together again was slim. He lived in Pennsylvania and she lived in New York.

As the plane slowed down in its taxiing, Ellis smiled at her. "It was really nice talking to you."

"My pleasure. You keep in touch. I want to know how your Panera people react to the big news."

"They'll be sad to see me go."

"I bet."

Finally, the plane stopped and people began to turn on their phones, stand to stretch their legs and reach for the bins.

"That's weird," someone behind Ellis said. "I don't have a signal. No bars."

"Me either," another said.

Ellis pulled out his phone and took it off of airplane mode.

No signal.

He was about to ask James if he had a signal, but James wasn't even looking at his phone. He stared intently out the window.

"Ellis," James said. "Take a look. This is weird."

"What is?"

"We're not at the terminal. In fact, I don't even see the terminal."

Ellis leaned over James to look out the window. Clearly, they were on a runaway, but there were no other planes. All he saw was an empty airfield He turned around to see if he could see through the window on the other side, but it was a large plane and those in the center aisle blocked his view.

"Maybe they're backed up at the terminal," Ellis suggested.

"So why aren't we waiting on the tarmac."

"Ladies and Gentlemen," the pilot spoke. "If I can have your attention."

Ellis pointed up. "He's about to tell us."

"We apologize for the delay. If you can just take your seats. We have a bit of a situation and I'll get more information to you when I can. Thank you."

That was it.

No real answers.

Ellis wondered if something had happened at the airport. Was there something going on in the city?

Even without the pilot saying anything more, Ellis deduced quickly that it wasn't the city or airport. The way the flight attendants huddled and whispered looking around, Ellis knew something was happening on that plane and hopefully, it would be over soon and he wouldn't miss his connecting flight home.

Little did Ellis know, that wasn't going to happen.

ELEVEN – SECRECY

He was so frustrated. Josh wanted to break his phone, then again, he couldn't. His communication with Jen would be few and far between because there was no signal where he took her in West Virginia. There was only a mere payphone, as if they were back in the 1980's.

He used the four and a half hour drive to D.C. to charge his phone, to communicate with his new staff in Washington D.C. and also to call Alek. But those attempts to reach him were futile. He left message after message, hoping that Alek would call him back. After hours of driving, he finally arrived and parked at the Pentagon where he assumed he would be meeting Lenore. At the gate he was directed to a wing that hadn't been used in a long time, and told he'd find parking in the smaller lot.

Just as he pulled in a spot with two armed guards by an entrance, his phone rang.

Finally. Alex was calling back.

"What is so important my friend?" Alek asked.

"Thank you for calling back. I need to know, did you have any contact with the man that took it?" Josh asked, keeping the details secret in case somehow they were able to tap into his phone.

"No," Alek replied. "He went back to his village in Germany right away."

"How did he get there?"

"My plane flew him and he drove the rest of the way, I assume."

"Alek, this is important, I need you to find out where he had been for the last twelve hours."

"Doctor Brayden," Alek said. "What's going on?

"He didn't do it correctly."

"What do you mean?"

"He went in to the chamber to place it in the container."

"He wasn't supposed to."

"No," Josh replied. "I gave specific instructions. He also cracked the window."

"Sweet Mother of God."

"Yeah. Right now, we are watching a woman survivor down there. I'm hopeful that she and the other man who made it to that level weren't close enough."

"But he was?" Alek asked.

"Yes."

"And this means what?"

"If we don't contain him. If we don't contain this, Alek, it's over. I would advise not leaving your private island at all."

"Thank you, Doctor Brayden. I will take care of it."

Josh ended the call and found it suspicious. Was Alek's demeanor that cool and calm that he didn't get upset or was he expecting the weapon to leak? Alek was the money behind the country that wanted YPP-234. The perfect buyer; a country that would never use it.

A worst case nightmare was unfolding.

Josh couldn't over think it. None of what happened was supposed to go down the way it did.

His claim to ignorance led to the potential undoing of civilization as he knew it. Josh never meant for it to happen. He didn't want those people to die or be shot, they even killed the contact inside that gave them the access to the biometrics.

They were supposed to storm in, get the weapon and storm back out.

Josh was supposed to get twenty-seven million dollars and live out the rest of his life happy.

There was no way he could change the course his greed had taken, but hopefully, it wasn't too late to change the path that YPP-234 could take.

<><><><>

When Josh went inside, it was evident the sealed off wing was in fact at one time a research center and possibly BSL4 lab. No one was there but his two new assistants.

They were in the large meeting room, which looked like a throwback to the 1970s.

It was easy to determine which assistant was who. A male and female. Cali and Roger.

Roger sat at the head of the conference table, Cali sat on the long side, both with two laptops before them.

Roger stood when Josh walked in. "Doctor Brayden."

"Roger," Josh shook his head. "Just call me Josh. And you're Cali?" he faced the young woman.

"I am," she replied. "Your issued laptop is there." She pointed to the other end of the table. "You have a video conference call in a few minutes."

"Thank you." Josh walked to the other end of the table. "Did you both get my research files so you're familiar with YPP-234?"

Cali nodded. "We did. I do have questions though."

"And I'll answer anything I can after the conference call," Josh replied. "I promise. Do we have anything? How is tracing?"

Roger replied, "Pretty good. We're not only getting everywhere her phone pinged, but wherever she used her debit card and credit card."

"That's excellent and fast, too." Josh sat down lifting the laptop lid. On the blank screen was a yellow Post it with his password and log in information.

"On the positive side," Cali said. "At the twenty-four hour mark she was at the hotel, got in a cab with Senator Morrows and went directly to the airport."

"Cab driver and Morrows?" Josh asked.

"Both have been placed in special quarantine," Roger answered. "The front desk workers and those in line from the video, we have sequestered. We are tracing the people on the plane."

Josh sighed out. "This is good. Good work" He looked down to the laptop when a notification for the conference popped up. "Will you two excuse me while I take this?"

Roger asked. "Do you want us to leave?"

Josh shook his head. "No, I may need answers. Stay."

The meeting fired up and the first video image was of Lenore. Josh wasn't sure where she was, there was a lot of background noise, but he was shocked when he saw the other attendee was President Conrad.

"We're not waiting for anyone else," said Lenore. "Doctor Brayden has a team in D.C. and we will get him to New York, because we have to follow this without missing a mark."

"Doctor Brayden," President Conrad said. "Give it to me straight. Are our efforts going to be a waste of time?"

"I certainly hope not," replied Josh. "I came to Senator James because I worried about something like this happening. And if you'll excuse my language, General Scott made me look like an asshole. A team that day, that last day of the hearing, should have gone into that lab and shut it down. Unannounced."

Lenore sighed out. "Word got out we were going. Honestly, if all those people hadn't been killed, I would have thought we went in and stole it back."

'We're tracing it," explained Josh. "If we can lock down everyone that's been exposed to Katie, we have a chance of containing this."

"What about the man that stole it? The one that grabbed the canister or cylinder?" asked President Conrad.

Josh answered. "I watched the video. He was wearing a mask and gloves, he could be protected. Our concern is Katie. Get everyone who was around her. It takes twenty-four hours for an individual to become contagious. So our clock is ticking. She became contagious at nine forty-five am central European Standard time. Which is six hours ahead of us."

"So that gives us approximately eight more hours to locate every one?" President Conrad asked,

"Yes."

"Everyone?" he asked again. "Every single person she passed, met, touched, bumped into. Impossible."

Josh lifted his hand. "Not everyone she passed or talked to will get it. It's not like a chemical agent where everyone around it gets effected. Yes, she is a weapon and everyone she infected therefore becomes a weapon, but ... exposure and infection rate is roughly fifty percent and there are some people who have immune systems that aren't going to get the bacterium, which is what this is."

"You know this how? From lab experiments?" asked the president. "Rats?"

"As I stated in the hearings, they tried to move YPP-234 before and it was disastrous, an outbreak occurred in a small village. We were able to stop it, but we did get data we needed."

"Tell me, Doctor Brayden, what does this weapon do to people? What are the symptoms?" President Conrad asked.

"It's a souped up version of the plague. Bubonic, or Pneumonic, or both. Symptoms can show as early as twenty-four hours, and that's best case. Because they never became asymptomatic carriers. But they can be carriers for up to seven days."

"How did you stop it? Contain it?" The President asked.

"Burned out the village," Josh answered.

"Jesus," gasped Lenore.

"That's not an option," said President Conrad. "Despite what my advisors are saying, I believe our best option is to let the public know."

Lenore shook her head. 'People watched those hearings. They didn't believe Doctor Brayden. But ... if we let them know YPP-234 is out, and they have been given the facts already by Brayden himself at the hearings, there will be no sugar coating it. In three hours, there will be total panic."

"We get the guard ready," President Conrad said. "Urge people to stay claim."

"Stay calm?" Lenore asked. "Stay calm, hold hands and sing

kumbaya instead of shooting their neighbors or panic shopping the shelves bare? No. We stick with the plan. See what happens on that plane. For all we know Katie may not be a weapon or a carrier. If in seven days if no one is sick with it, we're done."

"We'll know much faster," said Josh. "Someone will be sick sooner than later."

"Right now." President Conrad shuffled through papers. "We have the old FedEx hangar being transformed to a prison style, high security, quarantine zone. CDC trucks and mobile labs are rolling in. A plane with two hundred and seventy-five people sitting on a closed runaway at JFK. How do we explain that?"

"Easy," Josh replied. "We say it's a suspected case of Marburg. People can Google that and get scared, but they won't be nearly as frightened as they will with this weapon. They'll see we have it under control. We play it off as long as possible. Keep in mind, if someone gets sick, the clock resets for those passengers."

"Then what?" asked Conrad.

"Then it's either over in a week, or worst case scenario it's not." Josh said. "Let's just pray we find everyone."

TWELVE – THE PLANE

Baldwin, PA

Not that Bebe needed the reminder, but when her phone sounded off about picking Ellis up at the airport, she was already at the baggage claim area waiting for him. She thought it would be cute and brought him flowers.

He was supposed to land at the Pittsburgh Airport shortly after seven. Flight 612. When she arrived at the airport, it was minutes until his flight was to land, she waited by the escalators knowing he would have to come down that way. Everything was planned. She expected to get him home by eight and as a family they would have a late supper. She was so excited for him to come home, that when her stepson Deke showed up, she had him babysit while she ran to the grocery store for a special dinner. It would only take thirty minutes. Not that he wasn't responsible, but she didn't want Deke to feel he had to babysit. That was why she called her aunt Shirl to watch them while she went to the airport.

Hopefully, everything was alright at home and with Ellis.

When Ellis didn't check in during his layover at JFK, Bebe was a bit concerned. His phone went straight to voicemail and text messages never showed as read. Then she just assumed his flight from London was delayed and he had to rush to catch his connecting flight. She imagined him running through the airport in a panic.

JFK was a big airport.

At the bottom of the escalator, holding that bouquet, Bebe readied to see her husband and greet him with the biggest smile and embrace. She saw his flight had arrived. Soon throes of people, crammed on the escalators, descended her way. She stepped aside to look for Ellis, returning a smile to those who smiled at her.

She watched the people make their way to carousel K, the Carousel for Flight 612.

It had to be his plane, maybe another.

Ten, fifteen minutes had gone by and no one else came down the escalator.

Maybe she missed him. She walked over to the carousel.

"Excuse me." She tapped a younger man on the shoulder. "Were you on Flight 612 from New York?"

The man turned around. "Yeah, I was."

"Thank you."

It was the right carousel.

It was Ellis' flight.

No Ellis.

Bebe pulled out her phone, she knew it was on. No missed calls or texts. She immediately called her husband.

Again, straight to Voicemail.

"Hey, Ellis, honey, please call me. I'm worried. Thank you. I love you. Bye," she left the message and ended the call.

No sooner did she lower the phone it rang.

She sighed out in relief that Ellis was finally calling, lifted it, only to see it was Deke calling.

"Hey, Deke, Dad must have missed his flight," she said as she answered. "I don't know what to do."

"Bebe," he said her name with such seriousness.

"What's wrong?"

"Are you by a television?"

Bebe looked around. "No. I don't see one." She began walking around looking.

"Go on line. It's hard to explain, it should be right there. The news."

"Oh, God, don't tell me a plane crashed."

"No. It's ..."

"There," Bebe said, spotting a television by the Starbucks. "I see one. What am I looking for?"

"You'll know."

"I'll call you back. Keep trying your father for me." After getting an agreement from Deke, she hung up and walked to the television.

The image on the screen was enough for her to know it was what Deke was talking about. A lone plane on a barren runaway. The blurriness of the video was obviously shot from far away and zoomed in.

She couldn't hear it, the terminal was too crowded and noisy, but she could read the closed captions.

'For several hours now,' the closed caption read as she came in midsentence. "Some reports are saying at least six hours. That is unclear. We do know this, there is a lot of movement, lots of military vehicles and a reporter from CHN has stated they saw three CDC mobile labs driving down Airport drive. Again, we don't know the status of the passengers inside, what flight it is, everything is hush hush. But considering the military presence, the CDC and the abandoned terminal draped in plastic, it's scary and something right out of a movie.'

Bebe's heart sunk. She prayed it wasn't Ellis' flight out there on the runaway, but her gut instinct told her it was.

All she could do at that moment was try to find answers.

<><><><>

Seven hours and four minutes, that was how long Ellis had been on that plane, parked in the no man's land of JFK. Seven hours without a word of why, the pilot intermittently announcing he didn't know anything yet.

Was that the truth?

A packed plane, no AC. It was hot, tempers flared and people argued. The flight attendants stayed away and Ellis didn't blame them.

They would be targets for the angry passengers on the plane.

Even if a passenger didn't vocalize it, the tension was thick in the air. So they locked themselves away in the galley, serving nothing.

The first hour was rough, irritability and confusion on why they were there parked and why they couldn't get a signal on any phone.

The second hour rolled in and people seemed complacent as if they believed it wouldn't be much longer. Ellis was hopeful because people started talking and joking in that third hour.

Then it began.

Hour four everything unraveled. By the time the seventh hour of being on the plane rolled around, it was a virtual vat of bubbling negativity.

The sun had set outside, minimal emergency lights were on.

Ellis hated to think of what would happen next if they were on the plane much longer. He thought he kept his cool pretty well, Ossie did, too. Telling her granddaughter to settle down and what good would yelling do. It wouldn't get them off the plane.

She was right.

Something was definitely going on.

James fidgeted in his seat, he wasn't as calm as Ellis. He bitched a lot and for good reason.

"Can we get some water, please?" James shouted which then started a symphony of yelling from passengers. All screaming for water or food.

"Please calm down," Ellis told James.

"Dude, I am thirsty, this is inhumane."

"I get it. I'm thirsty, too." Ellis felt the tap on his shoulder and turned his head.

Ossie showed him two little boxes Ellis recognized it as a juice box, the name and description in Spanish, the picture of fruit gave it away. "Would you and your friend like one?" she asked.

"Oh my gosh, I would, but I don't want to take your drinks."

"Don't be silly. These were supposed to be a souvenir for

my grandchildren, but I think we need them. Take them." She extended them.

"Thank you," Ellis gushed in relief and gave one to James.

James looked around Ellis. "Ma'am, thank you so very much. This means the world."

Ossie smiled gently and sat back.

Ellis sipped slowly so as to make it last. Those few sips of the mango flavored drink were the most rewarding and refreshing, and it wasn't enough to make him have to run to the bathroom.

He went early on but the line for every lavatory was insane. It dawned on him maybe they were going into the restroom for the water.

The line was weird to him, blocking an aisle, annoying those who sat in the seats and were getting bumped.

Every once and a while it would get tense with people shouting 'hurry up'.

When he heard the tone from the speaker, signifying the pilot was going to speak, Ellis looked at his watch.

Nearly eight hours had passed, hopefully, the end was being announced.

"Ladies and Gentlemen, at this time ..."

The pilot began speaking but Ellis couldn't hear it because at that exact moment, massive chaos erupted near the front of the plane.

He heard a man shout something about, 'keeping it all for themselves,' then he heard the sound of banging, a scream followed by argumentative shouting.

A huge fight broke out.

If his yelling out for them to be quiet wouldn't add to the calamity, Ellis would have said to shut up. Didn't they want to hear what the pilot was going to say?

Suddenly two beverage carts, pushed by passengers appeared in the aisle and people just jumped up, racing in throngs to the front. Rushing to those carts like a stage at a rock concert, running over each other, pushing to get to the cart as if it were the last thing they'd ever get to drink.

It looked like an ant mound, everyone on each other.

Some man from the far right of the plane, wearing a dress shirt with the sleeves rolled up, walked over and started moving people from the mound. For every person he pulled back, two raced forward.

Then in what Ellis thought was an idiot move, he raised his arm and fired a gun.

Silence.

Not even the pilot's voice was heard over the speaker. Ellis guessed he missed the announcement.

"I am with aircraft protection operations," he spoke firm and with a British accent. "You will take your seats or face federal aviation violations under United States law. Take your seats. Now."

No one moved.

"Now!" he shouted more firmly.

As people began to disperse slowly, the lights went out on the plane. But the darkness was short lived when bright exterior spotlights blasted through the small windows of the plane, creating beams of light.

"Once, again," the pilot said. "Please take your seats. Authorities will board to escort you off."

Obviously, the fight and commotion caused Ellis to miss vital information, but judging by the spotlights, it was bigger than even he thought it was.

THIRTEEN – THE HANGAR

Not one to take the Lord's name in vain, the gasping, 'Jesus' slipped from Lenore's mouth when she arrived to the old airfield at JFK.

It was unlike anything she had ever seen. Not that she was on the ground during major outbreaks but the entire area, runway, hangar was transformed into a scene from the movie 'I am Legend'.

Almost as if at any time she'd hear someone call out, "Quiet on the set,"

The mobile labs, office trailers, tents and military vehicles were positioned on the other side of the newly erected high fence surrounding the perimeter of the hangar. A guard took position out front.

Spotlights lit up not only the entire surrounding the hangar, but in the distance, the plane as well.

In the back of trucks, the spotlight followed a pushback, tug truck towing the huge plane.

General Scott was there when she stepped from the SUV, he greeted her with a handshake.

"This way Senator." He led the way and pointed at a silver trailer. "We're meeting with Doctor Rebecca Obadia, she is the assistant director of the CDC, but has three plus decades of research experience under her belt. She is who we want."

Lenore slowed down as she approached the trailer. "Are the passengers still on that plane?"

"Unfortunately they are," he replied. "Everything is set up now, we just need to secure their entrance into the QZ. We want them in there before the residual onset. The shortest incubation period is twenty-four hours to symptoms. If your aide was indeed infected with the weapon, then we have, according to the video, one hour and thirteen minutes and we could see the first victim."

"That specific?"

"The weapon is that specific, yes." He opened the door.

As soon as he did, Lenore heard arguing. One voice she recognized as Doctor Brayden. But she knew he wasn't there.

"And I am telling you," Josh said. "As the designer of this monster, it is resistant to every strain of antibiotic out there."

"There has to be something." A woman sat in an office chair in front of a computer participating in a video conference with Josh Braydon. She wore blue jeans and a sweatshirt, sat in the chair, one leg bent up and her foot resting on the seat. Her hair was bright gray, nearly white, short, and when she looked over her shoulder at Lenore, it was hard to believe she had thirty plus years of experience, her face was very youthful. "Send me the slides and the images," she told Josh. "I need to know what we're looking at."

"Well, in about an hour, my guess is someone on that plane is going to show signs of infection."

"Such as?" Rebecca asked.

"It could be a number of things, it presents in several ways."

"That fast?"

"Let's hope," Josh said. "It's never been in the wild like this. We need to hope that somehow, this thing infects and shows fast. Otherwise it's going to spread like wildfire. Any news on grounding flights?"

Rebecca chuckled softly and sarcastically. "Unless we know for sure this Katie is carrying the weapon in her, nothing will be done."

"I drove just in case and will be there soon. Keep in mind, there is a chance she isn't carrying the weapon in her," Josh said.

"Let's hope. I will touch base here in an hour, right now I have General Scott and Senator James in here. See you soon." She ended the chat, swiveled her chair and stood. "Senator James." She extended her hand. "General."

"Please," Lenore said. "Call me Lenore."

"And me, Rebecca. Quite a risk coming here," Rebecca said.

"Well, I am responsible. Had my aide been one hundred percent honest this whole thing could have been diverted."

Rebecca tilted her head. "While I would like to believe that to be the case, I am not convinced this gunman who stole the virus isn't a weapon himself. If that's the case, all this could be for naught, if he is in the United States."

"Let's say," Lenore said. "Katie is not a weapon and all those people on the plane are good. But the gunman is, can we stop it from entering our soil?"

"Possible. If we stop all flights in. Those already in the air we quarantine, but we don't know who he is, so that puts us at a loss. We need to focus on here and now."

General Scott explained. "It will seem extreme. We have cut all signals on their cellular devices, no internet access, no means to contact the outside world. We're doing this to keep the calm. Once we get the passengers inside the hangar, we will reach out to the families and let them know their loved ones are safe. Initial quarantine is seven days, but if one person shows symptoms ..."

Lenore nodded. "The clock resets. Yes. I know we are operating under the guise of Marburg."

"Yes," Rebecca said. "And admittedly those in my field will see through it because this is extreme. I have never seen anything like it. I was told to imagine it was a highly contagious, airborne version of Ebola and what we would do. This is what I came up with. We are putting these people under lock and key, while trying to make them as comfortable as possible. They will receive food and books, entertainment means to pass the time. They can't leave. In fact, we are taking extreme measures so they aren't even close to the air outside the plane and hangar."

"And if someone does show symptoms," said Lenore. "You'll try to cure them?"

"To be honest," Rebecca replied. "We will make them comfortable. We're not here to cure them, I don't think we can. We're here to make sure it stops here and doesn't get out."

Lenore turned her head when she heard the heavy sigh. "General?" she asked. "What is it?"

"I think despite our best efforts here and now, sadly, it's too late," he said. "It's out. It's done. We need to focus on the aftermath. If ... there is even time."

<><><><>

Katie was singled out and with good reason.

Long before the plane landed, passengers in first class knew something was up. They had no idea they would be sitting on a runway for hours, nor were they told specifics, but how could they not know something was wrong. They knew before Katie did.

The flight attendant first approached the woman in the seat next to Katie. The woman stood and followed the flight attendant to the galley behind the wall. Katie couldn't see them talking, but knew something was up when they woman never returned. She sat somewhere else.

Katie assumed the woman wasn't supposed to be in first class, then the flight attendant approached the couple in the aisle across from Katie and the man behind her.

All of them had been moved.

In fact, they shuffled a lot of people around.

It was only when the flight attendant, wearing a facemask and gloves, and asked Katie to move to the front row, she knew what it was about.

They feared she was contagious with something. They were isolating her from everyone else. But how? She hadn't been in the lab where the weapon was held.

She tried to get a hold of Lenore via messenger, but her Wi-Fi was cut off. Others were using it, not Katie. Had Lenore found out she had been less than honest? It wasn't as if she lied, she just never told them where she hid.

Sometime after the flight attendant grabbed and bagged her finished tray, Katie was ignored. No drinks, no water other than the bottle she had with her. She sipped that, figuring no one wanted to get near her. It was a good thing she rationed the water.

Eight hours on a runway in a hot plane, no one in the main cabin was given anything out to drink. The flight attendants stayed near the front by the cockpit.

When night fell, things got crazier. She didn't hear the captain's announcement because of commotion behind her. There was even a gun shot. That happened before the plane powered down, went dark and was lit by bright spotlights.

People murmured around her, questioning what was happening, especially when the plane began to move slowly. The lights outside the plane prohibited her from seeing what was going on out there.

Then fifteen minutes after they stopped, the flight attendant asked everyone in first class to remain seated and stay back.

Two people in bio hazard suits then entered the plane. They wore large, green suits with helmets that looked like they belonged to spacemen.

No one said a word, not even Katie when the bio suit people approached her.

One was a man, his face illuminated by a yellow light inside his helmet. "Ma'am," he said. "Come with us."

"I'm not sick."

"Come with us."

Katie decided not to argue and stood. The moment she approached the door, applause rang out from first class.

They were happy their ordeal was over. Perhaps they thought they could go home. But Katie knew the second she stepped through the door of that plane, all the fuss wasn't just for her.

Katie wasn't the only one not going home, she just happened to be the first to leave the plane.

<><><><>

There was no engine noise, but the plane was moving. It moved at a slow pace, but the lights stayed with them.

The movement, the spotlights brought quiet to the plane as everyone seemed as confused as Ellis.

When the plane finally stopped moving, Ellis heard some sort of clanking outside, electronic, but he couldn't see.

"What do you think is happening," Ellis asked James.

James was staring out the window into the bright light.

"James?"

James sat up and wiped his eyes. "Sorry, I was staring out there."

"Well don't stare into the light, Dude, you'll hurt your eyes."

"Thanks, Dad," James joked.

"Are you alright?"

"Yeah, I'm fine. Tired. Hungry, thirsty."

"I feel you."

One hand on the seat in front of him, Ellis leaned toward the aisle to get a look.

Ossie asked him, "Do you see anything?"

"Nothing." Ellis inhaled deeply and sighed out. He felt like he was in one of those movies or TV shows featuring planes that he always watched.

There was one where a plane sat on the runaway in New York and everyone was presumed dead. Then another where everyone was dead on the plane and they didn't know it.

What if he was dead?

What if those spotlights were just lighting up the dead bodies inside the plane and like in that movie, he hadn't realized it yet?

It started to freak him out.

He wanted to talk about what was going through his mind, but he probably was the only one who thought that way.

A round of applause caught Ellis' attention and again he leaned into the aisle. "Something is happening."

"They are clapping and cheering," said Ossie. "I bet we're leaving the plane." He glanced back over at James. "Bet we're leaving soon."

James turned from the window. His eyes were red. "Hopefully, huh."

"I told you quit looking at those lights. Didn't you play that game as a kid?'

"What game?" James asked.

"See how long you can look at a light until you give up."

James chuckled. "No. No I didn't. "

Ellis shrugged. "I thought everyone did. What about the pixie stick game?"

"What is the pixie stick game?"

"Where you dump an entire pixie stick on your tongue and see how long you can go before swallowing. You know," Ellis said. "The sugar burns."

"What?" James laughed, then coughed once. "Oh my God, what the hell kind of torturous childhood did you have?"

"A lot more torturous than yours."

"We did that," Ossie said. "Not to eavesdrop. But I did that. You do crazy things to pass the time when you're poor and bored."

"Tell me about it." Ellis, repeating his earlier actions, leaned again, into the aisle. "Oh, we're leaving. Look, I can see first class walking out."

With a gasp of relief, Ossie placed her hand on her chest.

"Ladies and gentlemen," said the pilot. "We are now going to exit the plane. Please be careful moving things from the overhead bins, as items may have shifted during the flight."

That was it. No typical thank you from the pilot. Then again, he was probably as tired of being on the plane as Ellis.

The mood of the plane switched and people cheered,

standing up to start reaching for their bags.

Ellis and James were pretty far toward the back, and Ellis waited until the line moved. Other than the interior lights being off, everything finally seemed normal. Ellis just wished it wasn't so dark and he could see better. The spotlights really played tricks with his eyes.

Two rows before him, Ellis stood and waited for his carry on and James'. He helped Ossie with hers, then let her and her grandchildren go first. Stepped back, allowing James to go before him.

"Hopefully, I'll have a signal to call Bebe," Ellis said as they walked. The line to exit moved weirdly. Not steadily, it stopped every few seconds.

"I'm sure she knows," James replied.

Stop. Walk. Stop. Walk.

After a long, slow moving walk, Ellis entered the front of the plane.

Where were the flight attendants? Usually they stood there, thanking people, saying, 'ba-bye'.

It was at that moment, he heard Ossie's voice saying calmly, as she crossed the threshold. "It will be okay. Watch your step."

He couldn't quite make out what her grandchildren were saying. But the line didn't seem to be moving beyond her.

James made it to the door and stopped. "Oh man, Ellis. What the hell?"

Ellis saw it, too. They weren't crossing into a normal jet bridge that would lead them to a terminal, they had to walk down a flight of stairs, but that wasn't all.

The lights around them illuminated what was a tunnel of thick plastic surrounding the stairs and kept going, like tubes in a children's playground, only large enough to walk through.

"What is going on?" Ellis asked.

After the stairs and walking fifty feet, Ellis could see the end of the line. Never had it taken so long to deboard a plane.

A snail's pace walk, worse than the lines at Disney world. It had already been twenty minutes at least since he stood from his seat.

Ossie had to encourage her young grandson to move. "Come on," she told him. 'It will be fine. Grandma has been through this before."

"Ossie?" Ellis called her. "Do you know what's happening?"

"I think I do," she replied. "It's a quarantine."

Then just as she gave her answer, Ellis saw the frightening truth. At the end of the plastic tunnel were two doors. Before them stood two people in huge biohazard suits.

It was also the reason for the holdup of the line.

They'd stop a passenger, hold up what looked like an infrared thermometer, then after taking a reading, sent people through the door on the left.

There was no crowding by the doors, at least five feet separated the workers from the building. Enough room for them to check each person.

One by one, single file, Ossie and her family stepped up, the handheld device placed close to their head, a beep and they walked to and through the left door.

James stepped up.

The worker lifted the gun like object and paused for a second, before lifting and testing him.

No beep.

Instead a buzz.

The worker moved James to the side, informing him to step to the door on the right. He hesitated as Ellis was told to step forward.

James asked confused, "What's going on?"

"Sir, we need you to go in that door."

"Why is everyone else going in the other one?" James asked.

"Sir, please." The worker motioned to Ellis and lifted the readout gun.

As the gun beeped, and they told him to go to the left, Ellis was prepared to question why his friend was going somewhere else.

But the second he saw James, he knew why.

How long?

Twenty minutes.

Was it that dark on the plane that Ellis failed to see what was going on with James or did it happen so fast.

James' eyes weren't red from looking at the lights, they were bloody. His face was splotched and a deep purple ring formed under his swollen neck.

"Oh my God, James. What ..." Ellis didn't get to finish his sentence.

With eyes rolling to the back of his head, as if every support bone was pulled from his body, James dropped like a rag doll to the floor.

PART THREE

OUTBREAK

FOURTEEN – LOOKING THROUGH

JFK QZ – New York

Was James dying? Ellis wondered. He went between looking down to his phone for a signal and the time, to James laying on a FEMA cot. He couldn't believe what was happening.

His friend was just lying there. No blanket, shivering, laying on his side staring at Ellis. A plastic wall separated them.

A wall of plastic from the ceiling to a sectioned off third of the hangar that had been transformed into what looked like a refugee center.

Ellis really hadn't looked around much. There wasn't anything to explore. On his side it seemed empty. On James' side twenty or so cots were set up. James was one of three people laying down over there, and that woman. The young woman they let in front of them in line, she was cornered off in an area alone.

Isolated.

A long day which was far from over. His flight from London touched down at 4:40 PM. In his mind he believed he had to make the mad dash to catch his connecting flight home, which boarded in less than an hour after he landed. Ellis and James never made that flight. They never left the plane and when they did, it wasn't what Ellis expected.

His poor wife. She was supposed to meet him at the airport, how long did she wait? Did Bebe find out what was happening or know more than Ellis?

Nearly one in the morning and all Ellis wanted to do was call his wife.

"Ellis," Ossie gently called his name, placing her hand on his shoulder. "Your friend will be okay."

"They aren't doing anything for him."

"They wanted to separate the sick from the healthy first, they will," she said. "Right now you need to get your cot, your space and a box."

Ellis turned from looking through the plastic and faced her. "I'm sorry. What?"

She pointed across the hangar to a row of folded cot style beds. Each had a blanket and sheet folded on top. Next to each was a box. "The box contains toiletries, food and water. But the food is …" She closed her eyes to think. "They may be called MER? My granddaughter, Rosalie said the name."

"MRE," corrected Ellis. "Meals Ready to Eat. They're not wanting to come in here are they?"

Ossie shook her head. "Rosalie has claimed that corner over there to set up. It's private. Please join us."

"I will, thank you."

"Staring at your friend isn't going to help."

"I know. But I want him to know I'm here," said Ellis. "As soon as I see someone is tending to him, I'll join you."

"And you need to eat. Your mother would be angry with me if I didn't feed you."

Ellis smiled. "She would be grateful for all the snacks you gave me. Ossie?"

"Yes."

"You said something about being through this before."

Ossie nodded. "When I was very young. Five. My parents, my entire family, came from Cuba to this country on a very packed boat."

"Cuba?" Ellis asked. "When you said you were visiting family in Spain …"

"My husband's family. The great-grandmother of the

children."

"I'm sorry, I didn't mean to interrupt your story, continue," said Ellis.

"On the boat someone was ill. It was smallpox. A government ship intercepted us and saw the pox. When we arrived in America, we were placed in a place much like this. Shut off from everyone. Smallpox is very contagious."

"Yeah, I know," Ellis said. "How bad did it get? I mean, with the small pox."

"I lost my mother and grandfather and younger brother."

"I'm very sorry."

"Thank you."

Ellis looked at James. "This isn't smallpox is it?"

Ossie shook her head. "No, I can't even begin to guess what this is."

"How long were you in quarantine?" Ellis asked.

"A long time. Weeks. When we left, half of those there had passed away."

Ellis sighed out heavily. "Scary." He lowered his head. "Weeks. I just hope someone got in touch with my wife."

"My new friend. This isn't sixty years ago. I am certain," she said. "Bebe is aware of what is going on."

<><><><>

Baldwin, PA

Bebe's feet hurt so bad and not only was her body exhausted, she was mentally drained. Nearly five in the morning she dragged herself into the apartment with no more answers to what was going on with Ellis than when she arrived at the airport nearly ten hours earlier.

It was quiet in her apartment building. Bebe couldn't recall the last time she was out and about at that early hour.

She was surprised when she walked in to see the lights on. She expected her Aunt Shirl to be sleeping on the chair, instead,

Tammy, Ellis' ex-wife was there. She stood from the couch and rushed to Bebe.

"Oh, Bebe, I am so sorry you're going through this." Tammy embraced her.

"What are you doing here?" Bebe asked out of curiosity. There was never any animosity between the two women at all.

Ellis's ex-wife, and Deke's mother was a taller woman, more on the glamourous side. A high end fashion model in her younger years who turned into a lawyer. Beauty and brains and she was a nice person, too.

Tammy replied, "I was concerned and when Deke said your aunt had been here a while, I came over to help and to let her go home to rest."

"I really appreciate that." Bebe kicked off her shoes and dropped her purse on the chair. Her eyes shifted to the television. Images of the plane were still on the news as if the media was expecting it to do tricks. "I called a hundred places and nothing. I had to wait at airport security for two hours to get zero answers. Anything new on the news?"

"Nothing, but Daryl is out in the car. He has been on the phone with his cousin," she referenced her current husband.

"Oh, Tammy, he has to be exhausted," Bebe said. "Didn't he just get back from Germany before I left?"

"Hey." Tammy grabbed her hand. "He will do what he can. We all love Ellis. His cousin is the chief of staff to Senator Morrows. So, we're hoping for some answers."

"You think the Senator knows anything?"

"He's a Senator in New York," replied Tammy. 'I would think he knows about a plane sitting on a runway in his state."

"Thank you."

"I just feel so bad for all of you."

"You, too," said Bebe. "How does this happen?" she turned when her apartment door opened and Daryl walked in.

"Anything?" Tammy asked.

"Yeah." Daryl shut the door. "The plane is quarantined. He says a person in first class has Marburg."

Bebe shook her head. “What is that?’

“It’s like Ebola times ten,” replied Daryl. “But it was in first class, so Ellis was probably far enough away. Still they need to quarantine.”

Bebe gasped. “How long? Will I get to talk to Ellis?”

Daryl replied. “I asked him, but he didn’t know. He’ll find out, I promise. The news will break soon to the public. As soon as it does I am sure you’ll hear from Ellis.”

“You really think he’s okay?” Bebe asked.

“Positive.” Daryl pointed to the television. “This will be over soon.”

<><><><>

“It won’t be over any time soon,” Josh spoke to Lenore and Rebecca as he suited up on the other side of a window in the CDC mobile lab.

General Scott stood in the back just watching him without saying a word.

“As of now, four are ill.” Josh said. “That’s not even five percent of those exposed.”

Lenore asked, “Isn’t that a good thing?”

“No. No it’s not. Nearly three hundred people were on that plane. We have confirmed that Katie is a weapon. So at least half will get infected from her. I was hoping more would be ill now. “

“What?” Rebecca asked shocked.

“Again," Josh stated. “The shorter the incubation the more chance we have of stopping this. I’ll know how it’s progressing once I examine them. Have we heard anything from the contact tracers?”

Rebecca shook her head.

“Damn.” Josh grabbed his head gear. “Once the big wave hits in there we’ll have more of an idea what we’re dealing with and the time frame. I’m thinking two days. We’ll see.”

Lenore asked, “Will you be staying here in New York through this?”

“Yes,” Josh replied. “I know it’s dangerous. But I hid my wife away in the mountains of West Virginia. Holly River. Her health and safety is what matters most. I suggest you move your own families just in case."

"Thank you," Lenore told him. "Good luck in there."

Josh nodded then placed on his helmet and stepped out where he would be taped up and hooked to oxygen.

Rebecca sat down before the computer. "We'll be able to watch and hear everything from his camera. We are so lucky to have him."

Lenore agreed with a closed mouth look and nod. "And he doesn't have to. He could be in West Virginia with his wife. Very unselfish. Don't you agree General?"

General Scott just stared forward.

"General? Lenore called his name again.

General Scott snapped out of his daze. "I'm sorry I was just deep in thought."

"About Doctor Brayden?" Lenore asked.

"Yes. Because I'm curious," he said. "Just how sure are we that he isn't behind this outbreak?"

When he said that Lenore turned and looked at the stone faced General. "That is really a right field comment to make."

"Is it?" General Scott asked. "I told you at the hearing he was trying to sell that weapon. What if the entire lab takeover and mass shooting was the end result of a signed deal?"

"Why be here?" asked Rebecca. "If he sold it, he sold it for more money than he needs, why not be tucked away with his wife safely?"

"I don't know." General Scott shrugged. "Could be narcissistic, or guilt because he didn't expect it to get out, or maybe the villain longs to look like a hero. Whatever the case, I'd bet my three stars," he said. "He's behind it all."

From the time Josh left the mobile lab, it was twenty minutes until he was completely ready to enter the QZ. A lot of factors had played into the length of time. Most of which were to protect him from the weapon or carrying it outside.

During that wait, Lenore went to work. She didn't take it lightly what General Scott had said. In fact, she took it quite seriously.

Rebecca sat waiting on the video image. To her if Josh released the weapon at this point was irrelevant. If they didn't beat the crisis it wouldn't matter. Josh was the best hope, guilty or not, to beat this.

That was her main goal.

The general had left to make a few phone calls, Lenore assumed he was looking into things as she was. She didn't, as her son would say, 'piss around', she called a contact at the FBI.

And it didn't take long for the contact to get back to her.

Just seconds before Josh stated that he was in and the video feed of patients would start, the contact got back to her that Josh had received a large sum of money listed as a payroll deposit.

While it wasn't in the vicinity of 'illegal weapons sale' money, it was much more, ten times more than his normal pay deposits.

Telling her contact to keep on it, Lenore turned her focus to the video feed.

"He's in," Rebecca announced.

On the positive side, there were many more empty beds than ones taken. Was it possible, Lenore wondered that his Holy Grail of a weapon wasn't all that?

But the moment the video was on the face of a younger man, Lenore's heart dropped to the pit of her stomach. His head was turned sideways, eyes staring blankly out. Had he not blinked Lenore would have thought he was dead.

"My God," said Rebecca. "This is horrible."

"First victim," Josh said. "Is a man, appears to be in his mid to late thirties. No name. Medical team notes he has not responded to touch or sound. Vitals are low. Definitely presenting signs of YPP-234." His hand and video went to his chest. "Buboes are present under the neck. They are large and ..." he touched them. "Filled completely. Draining them may help." He examined him further. “Several buboes in the groin area. Body temperature is 103.7. He is unresponsive. Breathing shallow. Right now he is being given saline and the antibiotic Gentamicin, which isn’t going to work. I expect him to expire within a day.”

“Good Lord.” Rebecca sat back, shook her head, then spoke to Josh. “Doctor Brayden please remember this isn’t a lab, these are people. That is someone’s son, okay.”

“Heard,” he replied. “My apologies. I’ll move on to check the others. Were they all symptomatic when taken from the plane?"

"Yes, they were,” Rebecca answered. “And all seemed to be in the same stage. Is it possible that no one else will get it?”

“Possible not probable. We’ll know in two days. Not just here. Overseas, the person or persons that stole the weapon, anyone they came in contact with will be getting sick. I mean we have a real shot of containing this in the US. Katie was on a plane. We have them all.”

Lenore added. “And Senator Morrows has been isolated before his twenty-four hour mark.”

“Exactly,” said Josh. “So as long as he stays put and these people go nowhere, the buck stops here.”

“What about our patient zero?” asked Rebecca.

“The weapon,” Josh corrected. “She should start showing symptoms in five days. Seven at the most.”

“And if she doesn’t? Does that mean she beat it?”

“Hardly,” Josh answered. ‘If she never gets sick, that’s another bridge to cross. It doesn’t mean she’s no longer a weapon. Again, the buck has to stop here. Now, if you’ll excuse me I’m going to finish my assignments.”

Lenore watched him walk from the first patient and across the small ward. She looked down to Rebecca’s computer, “I know YPP is a souped up form of Bubonic plague. Why are we not testing them?”

“We are, but Doctor Brayden doesn’t think it will show a positive until symptoms are present.”

“I’m not a scientist or doctor,” said Lenore. “But am I correct in assuming it could very well be spreading on the healthy side of the QZ?"

Rebecca nodded. "More than likely."

"So why do we have the divided wall if we aren't doing anything to stop the spread?"

"It's more for the mental health of those not infected," replied Rebecca.

"So it's for show?" asked Lenore.

Again, Rebecca nodded. "And if Doctor Brayden's prediction is correct. In a couple days there will be nothing left to divide."

"In order for the buck to stop here, none of those people will ever get out of here? We just have to wait for all those people to die?"

Rebecca didn't verbally reply. But the way she exhaled and pursed her lips with a defeated expression, all but answered that question for Lenore.

FIFTEEN – OUTSIDE THE HUB

Holly River, WV

It was an absolutely beautiful fall day, ruined by the prospect of what could be when the alarm on Jennifer's phone went off.

She had set it according to Josh's request.

"Work on the assumption of the worst," Josh told her. "When that alarm goes off, it would be five days since the woman was exposed to the weapon. Four days since the weapon was activated in her. That alarm signifies seventy-two hours since we got her. If I am back, she wasn't infected and neither was anyone else. If I am not back. Assume it's not good."

It was confusing when he said it and Jen went through it in her mind, writing it down to make sense out of it.

They got the woman. Quarantined her and the others on the plane. Basically, Josh was saying if after three days no one was sick then it was done.

He'd be back.

He hadn't returned and being out of range with no internet, Jen was in the dark.

She only hoped he was running late. She wouldn't give up hope, not yet.

Needing something to take her mind off of her worry, Jen decided she would go fishing. Her father taught her well and she was quite good at it.

Plus, it was relaxing. The cabins on that part of the mountain were spread out. She hadn't spoken to anyone, seen no one, and was stuck inside her own head.

Fishing was the answer.

Depending on if and what she caught would depend on whether she would eat that or the meat in the freezer.

Down by the river, near the mouth of the small lake, Jen found her spot. She had been there an hour with no luck when she saw him.

At first, she thought it was a vision, an illusion or maybe even a ghost. How long had he been there?

She had been so in her own world, it took for an unsuccessful and frustrating reel for her to see him.

He took her breath away.

A young man. His thin statue, backwards baseball cap, his tan shorts and tee shirt which were not conducive for the chilly weather, made her wonder if she were seeing things.

She whispered out in shock, "Matthew."

Her son's name. The nineteen year old son she and Josh had lost. The young man to her right, at fifty feet away looked so much like her son.

Her heart skipped a beat. It was so uncanny, it could not have been real. The way he stood, cast his line, while a cigarette rested between his lips.

She was stuck in a mesmerizing stare of him. He noticed and lifted his hand in a wave.

It shocked her, made her heart flutter and she waved back.

"Doing any good?" he asked.

Jen didn't answer. She couldn't.

"Or not," he said.

"Sorry. I … you look familiar to me, I was just taken aback," she said. "No. No good at all."

"Yeah, me either. And I've been here at least an hour before you."

Was she so in her own world that she didn't see him when she showed up? Obviously.

"Last two days this place was kickin'." he said. "Wait. Whoa.

Got one." He laughed. "Wow, it's big. Dinner's on me."

Dinner's on me.

Hearing that sent Jen into an immediate memory of Matthew. He was barely fourteen and they had gone to Canonsburg Lake to fish. He was quite good and back in the day when she couldn't imagine he would be gone so soon after.

Actually, it was the day he died that Jen found out he had been using drugs. She never knew it. People asked her how she didn't know, but it was one of those things where she just subconsciously refused to believe it.

Josh knew, he tried to tell her and Jen denied it.

Maybe if she didn't go through with blinders on things would have been different.

"Sweet," Matthew chimed out as he lifted the fish. "It's a big one, too. Dinner's on me."

Jen laughed. "First of all Matt, you can't keep what you catch here. Second, that's a carp."

"Hello," the young man at the fishing hole called to her. "You okay?"

"Yeah." Jen smiled gently. "Was thinking of something."

"I'm sorry. I wasn't like hitting on you or anything."

"Oh my God," Jen laughed. "I know that. Plus you're the same age as my son."

"Is he here?"

Jen shook her head. "Nope."

"Anyhow," he walked over holding the fish. "This is huge. Fire pit is in the community circle, we can fry it up. No hitting on you."

Jen smiled. "I'm sure your parents or friends would appreciate sharing that with you."

"Nah, I'm by myself," he said. "And I'm not a serial killer. So don't be afraid. Okay, I wouldn't tell you if I was." He held out his free hand. "Monty."

"Jen." She shook it. "And are you running away? Like a retreat. It's just odd being alone here."

"No one is here."

Jen bobbed her head left to right. “Off season.”

He wasn’t asking who she was with and Jen wasn’t going to volunteer that information. She didn’t know him and alone it was dangerous. Even if he did remind her of her son.

“I think that’s why my dad sent me,” he said. “I never even heard of the place. We’re from D.C.”

“Your dad sent you here?” Jen asked. “You have to be like nineteen.”

“Dude! I am. Good call. Is that your son’s age?”

“It is. And you don’t have to tell me, but why did your dad send you here? Is he joining you?’

“Don’t know. Maybe. And you wouldn’t believe me if I told you. Not that I’m supposed to tell anyone.”

“That’s odd,” said Jen. “He sent you here and the reason is a secret.”

“Yep. He’s a big military guy in D.C. But I think he’s headed to New York now or in New York.”

“The plane?” Jen asked. “The one on the runaway?”

Monty didn’t answer, he bit his bottom lip, then cleared his throat. “How about that fish dinner?”

“Monty, you don’t have to confirm anything,” Jen said gently. “I’m here because my husband sent me here because of that same plane on the runaway.”

“No shit.” Monty nodded. “Gonna clean this fish.” He started walking toward his gear and stopped. “Would be pretty wild if your husband was Doctor Brayden.” Saying no more, Josh gathered his gear and headed back up the path.

Pretty wild, Jen thought. More than she realized.

<><><><>

Alek was a business man first and foremost, a rich one at that. He handled the negotiations for the transfer and purchase of YPP-234. Admittedly, he had a hard time believing Doctor Brayden. He played it off as he was concerned, truth was Alek thought Brayden. Had seller’s remorse. Then ten hours later as

Alek made his way to his private plane, he received a photo of the first victim with a text that simply said, 'you must find him.' Meaning the man that actually was hands on grabbing YPP-234.

He had never seen anything that visually frightened him. It was the moment Alek cancelled his flight, deciding to stay on his island and immediately put forth the effort in finding the man he knew only as Clay, last he knew, his pilot flew him to Germany.

That text and that image from Braydon came three days earlier and finally Alek got word from his chief of security, He summoned him immediately to his home office.

"Tell me you have word," Alek said to his security man, Donato.

"It was nearly an impossible trace. The whole system you have is built on anonymity."

"I am aware."

"Clay was the one that hired the other seven," Donato said. "He's done a lot of work for you, so I went back to past jobs. Long story short, we were able to not only locate four of the men, and one woman on his team. We now know that Clay lives in Arnis Germany, fortunately it's a small village with a population of three hundred. He lives in a flat near the pier."

"And the others? Their health?"

"Not sick. Not yet."

"And you spoke to them when?" Alek asked.

"Yesterday. We only just confirmed Arnis as the location today."

Alek shook his head and looked down to his phone. "We're not in the clear. Who do we have near Arnis?"

"I can get a team there within two hours."

"Good. Good." Alek nodded. "Make sure they know not to get close to him or anyone else in town. Tell them it's small pox or something. Try to find him without contact."

"Yes, sir," replied Donato. "And when we do?"

"You know what needs to be done."

"Even if he's not sick?"

"We can't take that chance."

"Roger that," Donato said. "I'm on it now."

"Donny," said Alek. "No one is to arrive on this island. Shut down the pier. You hear. We lock down. We treat everyone trying to get here as an invasion."

"Yes, sir."

"Have you left the island at all?"

"No, sir. None of my people have nor your house employees."

"I won't keep them prisoner," said Alek. "But if they want to leave they can, they just can't return."

"Right now we're good, right?"

Alek nodded. "We're locked down tight. No chance we have exposure. Let's keep it that way."

After Donato left, Alek sat down again at his desk, feeling much better about everything. He was confident. His island was remote and secure and in his mind there was no one that could possibly be exposed.

But he forgot one person.

His pilot.

His pilot had flown to Spain, picked up Clay, took him to Germany and returned to the island for Alek. And while Alek wasn't near the pilot, others were.

Alek's remote and safe island wasn't as safe as he believed.

<><><><>

Baldwin, PA

Bebe was so grateful for Deke. She would be lost without him. He was such a big help with the kids, and a sense of support for her. Bebe was emotionally holding on with everything she had. It had been days since she spoke to Ellis. No official confirmation came from anyone that he was on the plane. And a part of her really felt that lady from the CDC was lying when she said she was hopeful that the Marburg virus was contained and those on the plane could go home soon.

If it was that cut and dry, why did they cut communications?

Bebe was falling apart, she felt useless and things were about to get worse.

"You wanna grilled cheese?" asked Deke. "I got an extra,"

Bebe sat on the couch, holding a crumbled tissue, eyes fixated on the news waiting on something.

"Bebe?" Deke walked in, holding out a plate.

"No, sweetie, I'm good."

"You have to eat. Please. I made it with love."

Bebe smiled gently and took the plate. "Thank you."

"We have so much food here. We need to start eating it."

"That's your mom, she's so kind."

"Let's keep in mind, mom didn't go buy it, she has a personal shopping team."

"It's the thought." Bebe took a bite. "This is delicious."

"Thanks, so uh ... anything?"

Bebe shook her head. "CDC lady said so far only four have it and it's a matter of days waiting to see if the others are clear."

"That's good right?"

"No. I read up on this Marburg, if your father has it ..."

"He doesn't. He's fine. They just won't let them call because they need calm. Speaking of which, I'm gonna check the baby."

Bebe reached out, grabbing his arm. "Deke, your father would be so proud of you right now."

As soon as her hand released him, her phone rang. She saw immediately it was Tammy calling and she answered it with a tempered, "Hello."

"Bebe, listen to me, okay."

Why did Tammy sound rushed, frightened? What was going on? No 'Hello', no how are you?

"Bebe, personal shopping team will be by in an hour. They will be dropping off a very large order, and the order will be in boxes marked as arts and crafts."

"Tammy, you just sent food. We have plenty."

"No, you don't. Take the food, tell no one you have it. It's vital that no one knows you have food and water and other items."

"Tammy, there's no need—"

"Yeah, there is. Listen to what I am going to tell you," said Tammy. "You don't leave the apartment. You barricade yourself in there. You do not let my son out of there. You hear? At all. Six weeks is what I heard. You barricade in. Open the door for no one."

"What?" Bebe asked in shock. "What is going on?" She stood. "Please, you're scaring me."

"You should be scared. But I need you to be strong. The news is going to break at six."

"What news?" asked Bebe.

"Senator Morrows is dead. A nurse that was with him in quarantine has it. It's not Marburg on the plane, Bebe. It's a weapon. A biological weapon. That's the news that's breaking. Now they are going to tell you it is contained to that plane in order to stop chaos, but it won't."

"Is it contained to the plane?" Bebe asked.

"I don't think it is."

"How do you know? Did Daryl's cousin tell you something?"

"No, Daryl did. Remember he flew in the same day from Germany? Bebe, he's sick. Really, really, sick," Tammy's voice quivered. "I think he has it."

SIXTEEN – ONE BY ONE

JFK QZ – New York

James had died.

Not twenty-four hours after he had stepped off that plane, was Ellis' business partner dead. He at least was receiving some sort of medical care, but during it all, James never moved or twitched. It was as if this horrible illness completely paralyzed him.

Ellis was sleeping when James passed. No one told him he passed. In fact, no one moved James for hours. Ellis woke up and sat by that plastic curtain so his friend could see him.

It was Ossie who came and got him and told him she believed James was gone.

Did he know? Did he feel pain? He just dropped and never got back up.

Then the next wave began. People didn't drop like James, the illness crept up on them. A cough, tiredness, then 'bam', they looked like James and were moaning, crying for help.

They were sick and in pain and one by one, people in spacesuits came and took them to the other side of the plastic wall. Soon it went from just four people to fifty. Ellis suspected more would succumb.

"You need to stay away from everyone," Ossie told him. "Stay with us. We stay as a unit. When we go for food, we cover our mouths. Touch nothing."

Ellis understood.

He envied Ossie.

How was she able to mentally keep it together? Ellis was out of his mind with worry about his family. No one was telling them anything, there was no news, no phones and at least once an hour there was a fight.

One man just lost it. Fought with a guard, knocked down a worker in a spacesuit, tackled another guard and bolted out the door.

Like many others, Ellis raced to a window. Ellis could sort of see through it. The hangar was draped in plastic and it was like seeing through his grandfather's glasses. But the longer he looked out, the better he could make out images. Like Ellis, everyone wanted to see what would happen to this man.

Ellis filled with dread for several reasons. He didn't want to see them shoot the man. Would they? What happened if he did get out? What would happen to the world if he had whatever it was they were trying to contain?

It angered Ellis because if that man escaped, everyone was in danger.

Still a part of him cheered for the man. He made it out of the hangar.

What surprised him, there was no gun fire. No one shooting at him. Against the brightness of the spotlight, even with the plastic, he focused on the outline of the man running.

He was going to make it.

When were they going to stop him?

Just as Ellis had that thought, as clear as day he heard the buzz and snapping of electricity and the flash of lights.

"The fence," someone said behind him. "The fence is electric."

If that was true, no wonder they didn't stop him. A fortified fence was impossible to get over without being killed.

They were locked in like a band of murderers. Maybe that was what they all were. Because if this thing they were quarantined for was as bad as it seemed, if they got out, they could be delivering a death sentence to others, making them all potential murderers.

Too many people worried about what was going on outside the hangar, Ossie thought. They needed to worry more about what was going on in the hangar. If they were with family, they needed to take the time to absorb that love and take in the moments.

There wouldn't be many left.

Ossie had a hard life, she was never rich. She had three children and her husband died when he was forty. Working two jobs was commonplace for her and finally, like with her new friend, Ellis, things were looking up when it all happened.

But instead of thinking, 'it figures', Ossie needed to be grateful for the moments and good that finally started to happen.

She wasn't alone, like Ellis. She had her grandchildren, Rosalie, Dane and Carlie. Rosalie was older, but the other two were so young. Dane was nine and Carlie was five. Everyone thought she was nuts taking them for so long and overseas. But Ossie could handle it, plus she had Rosalie.

Now the young ones were a blessing. They had a keen ability to block out what was happening and focus on passing the time. Rosalie didn't. She paced a lot, she kept wanting to go look out that small window.

"Gram, something is happening out there with the man who escaped," Rosalie said.

"And what can we do about it?"

"Don't you want to know?"

"No. Because doing so means crowding in with others. You saw how many people took to the other side today. Each hour it's more people. Don't let it be you."

"It won't be."

"I mean it. My grandchildren are my life. If something should happen to you, I won't survive it." And as those words slipped from her mouth, Ossie wanted to kick herself. Did she just foreshadow her own fate? In a time such as the one they were in, she very well could have. "Sit, Rosie."

Rosalie exhaled and sat down. "Oh, here comes Ellis. He'll know."

Mimicking almost the same exhale as Rosalie, Ellis sat down on the floor. "So, he was ... electrocuted by the fence."

"Whatever this is," said Rosalie. "It has to be so bad."

"No kidding, and I am not being sarcastic." Ellis turned his head to the sound of commotion.

A few men were scuffling, chest bumping and shoving.

Ossie shook her head. "They should be worrying about their health. Staying healthy and staying alive until we get out of here."

"Will we?" asked Rosalie.

"We have to," said Ellis. "Right? We all aren't gonna, you know." He made a throat grunting sound so as not to say the word 'die'.

Ossie understood what he meant, she nodded and turned her head to Rosalie when the young woman made a soft, 'oomph' sound. "What is it?" she asked her granddaughter.

"I just got really nauseous all of the sudden."

Ossie didn't worry about hearing that. She knew by looking at those who had gone down with the bug it was more flu like with fever, swollen glands.

"Did you eat the Chicken ala king?" asked Ellis. "It didn't sit right with me the other day."

Rosalie shook her head. "No, I had the stew." She grimaced. "I don't know ..."

The undeniable, loud thumping gurgle of her stomach rang out, sounding much like a flopping fish.

Rosalie's hand shot to her mouth. "I can't. I don't ..." Her shoulder lifted as she fought the retching. She jumped up and ran across the hangar, hand to mouth, to the small, two stall rest room.

Both Ellis and Ossie stood.

"Ossie, want me to check on her?" Ellis asked.

"No, stay with the little ones. I'll check on her. I'm sure it was something she ate." Feeling confident her granddaughter was fine and her body was just ridding the bad food, Ossie walked to the rest room.

The door was open, exposing the two stalls, one of which was closed.

"Rosie?"

"Grandma, help me. I'm so scared."

Another round of vocal heaving was followed by the sound of something rapidly pouring into the bowl. "Rosie, honey, I'm sure it will be fine."

"No. Oh my God. What's happening?"

"Honey." Ossie placed her hand on the stall door. It was unlatched and it opened immediately.

Rosie was partially sitting on the floor. Her arm on the commode and head on the rim.

Without hesitation, in a panic, Ossie cried out. "Someone. I need help."

Ossie wanted to scream out, cry, because she knew it wasn't food poisoning.

Everywhere in the bathroom stall was covered in blood.

SEVENTEEN – THE PEAK

Arnis, Germany

It was quiet. Even at a distance.

When Gerard, an investigative epidemiologist from Germany's Health Services pulled close to the water village of Arnis, he did so on a small ship with a limited crew, all ready to step foot in the town.

He could sense the quiet, the silence, not even the sound of birds were heard.

They hadn't a clue what they were dealing with or what happened.

For all Gerard knew it could have been a gas leak.

Authorities were alerted by a hysterical woman on a bicycle who had gone to Arnis to deliver a gift basket. She was screaming at the top of her lungs, "The town is dead, the town is dead. Everyone is dead."

The woman was admitted into the hospital for shock and trauma, unaware she wasn't the one who first discovered the bodies. Gerard would never know that a team of four men in search of a man named Clay would have entered the town to find everyone dead. Those four men in a twisted way, instead of calling authorities themselves, ordered the gift basket to be delivered.

Then after being exposed to the town, the men left.

It was hard for anyone to believe a whole town was dead,

even one with a small population.

A drone camera flying overhead confirmed there was no movement, no signs of life.

It wasn't as if the town actively communicated with anyone. Gerard wasn't familiar with Arnis. However, upon quick research he found out it could be upwards of a week for news to travel from or about Arnis.

If the town was indeed dead, they could have been dead for days.

They pulled up and docked, then suited up. It was the first time Gerard ever came in on a boat. They could have driven, but an alert had come from WHO, the World Health Organization, to be on the lookout for Marburg cases.

How someone in such a small town would get it, Gerard didn't know. People there generally stayed in their area.

Marburg was deadly, in fact, if a person caught it, there was no treatment. At over a ninety percent fatality, it was scary. Still, it wasn't as contagious as it was played off. Especially with the plane that landed four days earlier in New York.

He didn't understand why they had such an extreme quarantine. Unless it was a mutated form, something new or something secret.

Gerard knew Marburg well and there was no pulling the wool over his eyes with it. He had been on several outbreak sites. He knew it took very close contact to catch it.

With twenty-eight minutes of oxygen piping through his suit, Gerard made a call to his team through the suit radio to head back to decontamination at the ship in twenty-two minutes.

"Clock starts now," said Gerard, pairing off the eight of them in teams of two, each going their own way, routes predetermined when they were on the ship.

Gerard's path would take him to answers almost immediately.

After stepping on to the dock, there was a dock house, but no one was there. No one manned the boats or were out ready to go fishing.

Then again, it wasn't a surprise to him. The drone footage showed an empty town.

Had it truly been a gas or chemical leak, surely there would be someone laying in the street. But there wasn't.

Not fifty feet from the pier was a small café with a large front wrap around porch. It looked like a home was on top, a staircase led to an upstairs back entrance with a small porch landing and wreath on the door.

Gerard was going to head there, up the stairs, when he spotted what looked like an older and bigger gentleman seated on the porch in a rocking chair covered in a blanket.

His one hand rested on top of a mug on a small table as the man looked out.

Not once did the man turn his head or acknowledge the presence of people in biohazard suits.

Gerard realized why when he drew closer. The older man had passed away.

He probably wasn't a large man, he was slightly bloated in a post mortem condition.

He had been dead, Gerard guessed only a day.

The iris of his eyes were gray and clouded, his face, while decomposing showed the evident signs of what took his life.

The man's neck was purple and swollen twice its size with huge bulging, enlarged glands on both sides on his chin. Glands filled with a fluid wanting to burst out like an overdue pimple.

With his mouth partially open and tongue hanging out, Gerard knew what took his life.

He was strangled by his own neck condition, unable to breathe or swallow.

A horrendous, painful way to die.

And Gerard also knew one other thing. It wasn't Marburg that took this man's life. Like something out of the pages of a Black Death novel, the man on the porch died, quiet, evidently of … the plague.

Holly River, WV

Jen was hung over. It had been years since she drank so much that, despite how much water she consumed, she felt it the next day. The last time she felt so badly was after she and Josh attended a wedding and she swore then, she'd never drink that much again.

She hadn't.

Until that fish dinner in the community firepit with Monty.

Jen had a few bottles of wine and a fifth of bourbon, and if she wanted to enjoy them for the long haul, she had to ration. She made the mistake of telling Monty, at which, he ran to his cabin, three hundred yards away and returned with an unopened bottle.

Not that he drank, he didn't, but it belonged to his father.

Monty.

On the steps of her cabin, Jen sipped on her steaming cup of coffee and thought of the young man she had met the day before. He reminded her of her son Matthew so much Jen wondered if that was why she wanted to spend time with him.

There was a big difference between the two of them.

Matthew could not keep a secret. He was just like Jen. No matter how big or little the secret, Matthew like Jen could not keep it in. It screamed to come out. Jen always felt if she told just one person that the 'need to release the news' urgency would leave.

Matthew would always be like, "Mom, guess what? I'm not supposed to say anything, but you don't count, you're my mom." Then he would proceed to let the news roll.

Monty was either the greatest secret keeper of all time or he had keen, sneaky, interrogator abilities.

After their dinner, they both danced around the subject of why they were there, if either one of them knew about what was really going on at JFK.

Jen was good. She held back. Maybe that was why he gave her the booze. Lucky for her, she took that bottle back to her cabin and passed out in the chair.

Now she was paying the hangover price.

She thought about how silly she would sound if she was totally wrong about Monty. After all, what were the odds that his father was with Josh?

He never really said it.

It was Jen who made the comment, he merely replied that it would be wild.

"Stupid," Jen whispered to herself. It was that internal need to spill a secret and to talk to someone about it.

"Morning," Monty said in the distance.

"Hey." Jen looked up at him, he carried his fishing gear. "Are you hitting the spot?"

"Yeah, you wanna come?"

"I'll pass for now."

"Dude, you look hungover."

"I am."

Monty laughed then drew serious. "So, can I sit with you for a second?"

"Sure." Jen scooted over.

"I need to apologize to you," he said as he sat down.

"Why?"

"Because I wasn't honest. I could tell you wanted me to open up, to admit to knowing something."

"Monty that is your call. Your business."

"Well, it's not right. Right now, you and I are the only ones in the campsite because my father bought out the other four cabins. Right now, we need to rely on each other. We don't know how long we'll be up here."

"Yeah, I was kinda hoping it wasn't going to be that long."

"Your husband is Doctor Joshua Brayden, right?"

Slowly, Jen nodded. "How do you know?"

"My father is General Montgomery Scott. He's with your husband now. I spoke to him."

"Your dad?" Jen asked. "How?"

"I have a satellite phone."

"Has he given you an update?" Jen asked, perking up. "Are things okay?"

Monty shook his head. "Jen, no. They're the opposite. My dad just told me ... it's bad. And things," he said. "Are about to get worse."

<><><><>

Other than the restroom, Rebecca hadn't left the chair in days, she slept in that chair and ate in that chair. Her focus was watching not only the images of those in quarantine, but reviewing slides of the samples taken from those.

There was such an air of sadness in that CDC mobile lab. Despite the lack of detection of the super bacteria in blood, the positive news was it had been detected in some glandular and sputum samples.

Results they didn't share with the asymptomatic victims.

It was all falling down.

One of the images that interested Rebecca most was that of Katie. According to Josh, she should have been sick, she wasn't. While the far end of the spectrum gave her two more days, something inside of Rebecca told her the young women that brought about so much death through her simple, naive, deception was never going to get sick.

In her own plastic bubble, she was destined to watch the world end.

Where did they go wrong?

Every single worker, every single soldier was confined to the QZ. They may not have been in the hangar, but they were forbidden to leave.

At least until it was all over.

Four workers had shown symptoms and after doing so, entered a special trailer.

No doubt, like dominoes they would all fall.

They failed to keep the bug in the hangar, God willing, they'd at least keep it in the zone.

So far she hadn't received any word of the contagion being anywhere else. She had to hold to that. That somehow, even though it seeped out, they were able to stop it right there.

Even if every doctor, scientist, nurse and soldier died right alongside those passengers, it was far better than everyone in the city dying.

"She's still not sick, I see," said Lenore.

Rebecca hadn't even heard her enter.

"Not yet."

"How long?"

"Two days," Rebecca answered. "Two days for everything and everyone and we will know."

"Will she get sick?"

"I doubt it."

"What does that mean?"

"It means she is the ultimate weapon. No one would ever know she was delivering a deadly dose."

"For how long?"

"I don't know. We ran DNA testing and are still waiting on results." Rebecca exhaled.

"My God," said Lenore. "You know it's six now."

"It'll grow."

"But if our workers and those of us here are exposed, then no one stands a chance."

Rebecca hesitated before answering. "I won't say that. I think of my mother."

"What do you mean?"

Rebecca recounted. "When I was young, my mother would always say she never got strep. That somehow she was immune to it. She could be next to someone with it, share a glass, she never got it. I thought she was crazy. After all she caught every cold or flu going around. When I became a scientist, she brought it up again and I decided to test her theory."

"And?" asked Lenore.

"And it was as if her body wouldn't let that strep in. That bacteria didn't stand a chance with my mother's immune system. Viruses invaded her. Bacteria, nope. Nearly three hundred people entered that hangar. Two or three will undoubtedly still be standing when it is all said and done."

"Including Katie?"

"Should she be standing? I mean if we all die and she gets out."

"She'll always be a threat."

Rebecca nodded and slowly turned around to face Lenore. She stood close to the door, away from Rebecca and wore a face mask. As soon as she got a good look at the Senator, her heart dropped. Lenore was pale, her nose and eyes red and the discoloration started around her neck. "You too?" asked Rebecca.

"You?"

Rebecca nodded. "My symptoms haven't started yet, it's in my glands."

"How? How is this happening?" Lenore stepped closer.

"I don't know. But like me, everyone else will start feeling it soon."

"The General?"

"Fine. His blood and cultures are fine. He's looking for Josh right now."

"What do you mean?"

"We haven't heard from Josh in over an hour, General Scott was getting worried," explained Rebecca. "He has to be somewhere, he is at the QZ."

"Could he have left?"

Rebecca shrugged. "The fences are all electric. The only way he would get out is if someone let him out. But there are orders that people have not to let anyone out. No one is to leave. None of us."

"It's still light out. Maybe he decided to take a nap," Lenore suggested.

The door to the trailer opened and General Scott walked in. "We have problems."

"Yes, we do," said Rebecca. "Both of us are infected, you shouldn't be in here."

"It doesn't matter. I'm gonna get it anyhow." General Scott handed over a tablet. "Look at this footage. Press play."

Rebecca took the tablet, the image showed a car near the gate. She hit play and it showed the car going through. "Oh my God. He left."

"Yeah," said the General. "Now click next. That is footage of him in his lab."

Rebecca watched only a few seconds and paused it. "He looks sick."

"He is sick. I just quarantined the guard who let him through. He said he looked sick," said the General.

Lenore gasped. "And he's out there?"

"Ma'am with all due respect, in about twenty-four hours, this whole quarantine zone is going to be useless. I'm not a scientist, but I can see this happening. There are too many holes, too many people slipped through our fingers."

"Are you saying we shouldn't worry about him?" asked Lenore.

"It doesn't matter to the general public, but it matters to me," replied General Scott. "I believe I know where he is going. I would like very much to find him and stop him. I am convinced he is going to find his wife. And that concerns me because his wife right now is in the same place as my son."

Rebecca heard him and understood. He wanted to leave and trusted the general would speak to no one and stay on mission. Find Joshua Brayden.

More than anything, Rebecca knew she was defeated. It was out. Why keep the quarantine going? She could just let those people in the hangar go. But they'd go home to their families, to their loved ones, and if there was the slightest chance their loved ones were safe and could be infected by the hangar people, it was a chance she couldn't take. It was a big chance. Her data combined with her knowledge, told her ninety-eight percent were infected.

In a couple days, those uninfected were going to wake up to their worst nightmare.

EIGHTEEN – FALLING

JFK QZ – New York

It just seemed to happen faster by the hour. When Ossie's granddaughter fell ill, she seemed to be the tipping domino, one by one, from bloody vomit to phlegm filled coughs and swollen necks. People dropped from the illness.

Ellis was still not sick, he expected to be. Perhaps he would be the last wave of the mighty to fall.

When he was fifteen years old he broke his arm when he fell off his bike on a trail. His parents, of course, took him to the emergency room. It just so happened that day there was a major accident involving a bus and several cars. Ellis remembered the emergency room that day. The mayhem, the groaning, crying, screaming and fighting.

It was so loud. He was glad his father ended up leaving. Not because of the noise, but because they had those people from the accident to treat.

In the hangar it was very reminiscent of that day. The noise level was unbelievable. There were some so sick, like Rosalie, they didn't move. Others were angry and fighting.

He didn't blame them. He was angry as well. No one told anyone what was going on, and as each hour passed, less and less workers came in.

It came to a point that Ellis couldn't take it anymore. Instead of fighting and getting angry, he just wanted to run.

The cries of pain from people who were losing loved ones and the moaning of the sick. The screaming of the belligerent and fighting was over the top.

He hated leaving Ossie, but he couldn't handle it. When he looked at her cradling her youngest granddaughter while Rosalie leaned against her, it was far too much. When he saw them, all Ellis could think of was Bebe and his children.

He thanked God they were safe, and whatever was making everyone drop like flies was confined to this hangar.

Or was it?

He didn't know because he hadn't a clue what was going on. There was no internet, no phone.

Finally, Ellis broke.

He couldn't watch the pain on Ossie's face any longer or stand the smell of the sick, and Ellis became like every other able bodied person, he raced toward the door. The mob of thirty or so people crammed there like a mosh pit, yelling and pushing.

Soldiers in gas masks and rubber style suits pushed their way in, using their rifles to move people back.

"You can't go anywhere!" yelled one of them. "None of us can. Stay back."

Bang. Bang, Bang.

Gunshots rang out. Ellis didn't see anyone fall, but he heard the screams, and then a group of men rushed for the door, moving the soldiers back and forth as if they were beach balls.

They made it out.

The door was still open, and Ellis, like them, fled towards it.

At that point he didn't worry about being shot. He didn't think of anything but going home.

It felt good to be out of there. Ellis actually paused to breath in the fresh, cool air that didn't smell of sour copper.

He felt the jolt as a couple of other people bumped into him in their run.

They were all running for the fence.

"I got to get home, I have to get home," Ellis thought. "I have to get there before this sickness gets out."

Stop.

Ellis halted in his run.

What was he thinking?

He wasn't sick, but that didn't mean he wouldn't get sick.

He very well could be a carrier like that girl in the plastic room.

If Ellis wanted to protect his family then he had to stay away from them. At least until he knew he wasn't sick or going to get sick.

Others knocked into him racing for the fence.

Ellis just stood there. Taking in the fresh air and watching them.

They screamed out, as if escaping prisoners saying, 'we're free, we're free.'

Ellis had forgotten about what happened to the last person that tried to make it out. Then again, all he saw was a blurred vision of what he thought was happening.

Then without the visual edit of the plastic sheath, Ellis saw firsthand what happened to those who tried to leave.

At least ten people made it to that fence at the same time. All jumping for it in an attempt to climb out. The moment they touched the fence ...

Pop, crack, sizzle.

With puffs of smoke, flashes of light, the people flew off and back, their bodies on fire as they landed on the ground with a hard thump.

One through ten, all of them died.

Two more couldn't stop in their momentum, reaching the fence as well, and met the same fate as the others.

No one ran to them to help or bothered to put out the flames. He supposed they were already dead from electrocution because no one could be ablaze like that without screaming in horrendous pain.

Sick or not, Ellis was going nowhere.

If he made it through and didn't get sick, he knew he would never see his family until that fence was down.

By then, who knew what kind of pandemonium state everything and everyone beyond that fence would be in.

<><><><>

General Scott took an unethical route to leaving the QZ, he wasn't really any better than Doctor Brayden. But he had to go. At least he took insurance. He grabbed a rabbit from the CDC lab, one that had not been exposed. Rabbits were the one animal known to die twenty-four hours after exposure. General Scott placed it in the back of Roy's car. Roy was his unethical means.

A specialist with the Guard, not sick, at least not yet. Roy had been working the gate and Scott made a deal with him.

"Get me out and you come with me. I know you're from West Virginia, that's where we're headed."

Roy happily agreed.

There was one other part of the deal. Because of what they were dealing with, Roy could not get closer than ten feet to his family for one week. Especially if the rabbit died.

After General Scott found Brayden, and he took care of that situation, he would do the same when he found his son.

Stay clear.

Their escape from the QZ timing was impeccable, as soon as they made it across the bridge into Staten Island, traffic started to thicken.

A seven hour trip would take them close to ten hours because of the time the two spent in traffic getting on the highway just outside of New York.

It seemed as if everyone was trying to escape, there was some major exodus out of the city, like a bad sci-fi movie.

Roy wanted to put on the radio, but General Scott wanted to reach his son first.

Finally, just outside of the state of New York, he did.

"Why weren't you answering?" he asked Monty.

"Dad, I was fishing all day. I didn't think you were calling back."

"Listen, I am on my way to you. I am going to have to hike it up the mountain that will take me several hours. But I should be there right after nightfall."

"Is that a good idea?" asked Monty.

"I'll keep my distance. But I'm not your problem," said the General. "Doctor Brayden is in route. He's infected and you must do what it takes to keep him away."

"Oh my God."

"Tell his wife. He is sick. Stay clear of him. Hopefully, we'll get him first. There's only one way in and out of that campsite. So if he's driving you'll know. If he's on foot. He'll be too sick to make it."

"Dad, we can't get the news or anything. What is going on?"

"Son, I'm not sure. But I do know this, our efforts to keep it in the QZ were in vain. I think it broke boundaries before we quarantined the first person. I'll let you know what I hear."

"Dad, be careful."

"You as well," said the general. "And remember. Whatever it takes."

When he ended that call, Roy immediately put on the radio.

It seemed as if in the snap of a finger, everything just imploded. The news were talking about a global biological weapon crisis. Explaining how there was an accident and pleading with the public to remain calm.

If they could, stay inside and away from people. The warning to stay clear of crowded areas explained the amount of traffic leaving New York.

The news was also imploring people that if they were sick, to stay away from other family members who weren't, and do not seek medical attention.

Medical attention would come to those that were ill.

Refugees centers were being set up by FEMA for those who were unable to stay locked down for three weeks.

The president urged people not to rush to the store, not to loot or panic.

General Scott imagined no one would listen.

He hoped that the measure would contain it.

Despite what Brayden said, there was no way something so

deadly could sweep across the globe and get everyone.

Only those truly exposed, like him and Roy.

During their hours in the car, the General kept checking on the rabbit. It was still alive, that was a good sign.

Roy's home was farther south in West Virginia, and he would leave General Scott on foot twenty miles from the camp entrance. That was close enough, Scott was in good enough shape he could walk that uphill, winding mountain road.

While in the car, General Scott changed from his uniform and made sure everything including his weapon and rations were in a backpack. He didn't want to look like military.

He wasn't there on a military mission, he was there as a father taking care of something vital for his son.

Scott had faith in his son. Monty wouldn't piss around if he saw Brayden.

Just before getting out of the car, General Scott wished Roy good luck and checked on the rabbit once more.

Perhaps he'd spot one on his walk, make his own test rabbit system.

Still the rabbit was fine, six hours after putting him in the car.

Little did General Scott know, the rabbit would be dead within four hours. Who passed on the illness, Scott or Roy remained to be seen.

In his hike up the first mountain, General Scott stayed close to the woods and avoided going near the property of any residential structures.

There were three mountain passages to go up and down before the final one that would lead to their camp site. At least that was what the map showed.

Somewhere near the third and final winding road, at least fifteen miles into his walk, General Scott spotted the car.

The same gray car that Brayden had taken to leave JFK. It had government plates and was pulled over to the side of the road.

He hoped to find a dead Brayden inside, that maybe the doctor had pulled over and died. Instead, when he peeked in the windows of the closed vehicle, he saw empty bottles of water on the seat.

General Scott didn't open the door. He made the assumption the car ran out of gas and Brayden got out to walk the rest of the way. What he couldn't assume was Brayden was too sick to walk the rest of the way.

Knowing they were both headed in the same direction and to the same place, General Scott picked up a daunting pace in hopes that a sickly Brayden was slow and he'd catch him before he made it to the camp.

Cabin Six was empty. It smelled musty from not being in use during the off season and though cold in there, Monty argued with Jen about why they would not light a fire.

Not until they knew the situation was over.

"Why here?" Jen asked.

"Because he knows which cabin you're in. This is a good distance away from it. No heat means no smoke signals. This won't last long. I feel it will be over very soon."

"I don't understand. Maybe if I talk to him," said Jen. "Are we even sure he's on his way?"

"More than likely he is."

"Why would he do that?" Jen asked with passion, pacing some. "He knows this virus. Why would he risk passing it on to me?"

Monty shook his head. "I don't know. Jen, how bad is this thing?"

"YPP-234? Bad. From what Josh told me."

"Why would he create something so bad? Why would he do that?"

"It was his job. He once told me scientists create worst case scenarios to learn to beat them in case nature throws one at them or somebody uses it as a weapon. But he couldn't do this. This was a Frankenstein monster. From what I understood, it grew out of control on its own."

"He knew it was going to get out of control, that's why he sent you with all that food."

"He said weeks. Not to leave for weeks." She walked to the window. "Which is why I just can't understand why he would come up here infected. Are we sure he has it?"

"Even if he doesn't. He's been around it," Monty answered. "He needs to stay away."

"But you said your father is on his way. Isn't that the same thing?"

"I can promise you, we won't see my father until he knows he isn't sick or, well, worse. We won't see him. And if I know my father," Monty said. "He'll handle this situation."

"You must be very close to your father."

Monty joined her by the window and chuckled softly. "Hardly. I wasn't always a good son. I caused him a lot of grief. Still, you know, no matter what I did, he was there for me, he would do anything for me. I never understood that."

"I do," Jen replied. "It doesn't matter what you do, say, or act, he is your father. A parent does anything to protect their child."

"You don't think he's going to try to find your son, do you?"

Jen gazed at him with sad and glossed over eyes. She hadn't told Monty the truth about Matthew, she didn't see a reason to. "I think in his own way, Josh is trying to get to Matt. But he's coming here first."

She saw the confusion on his face and didn't elaborate, she just returned to staring out that window and waiting for the Sat phone to ring. She loved her husband very much, mistakes and all. She didn't want him to suffer, all she wanted was for it to be over.

It would be.

<><><><>

"Brayden," General Scott called out his name in a firm manner, yet soft. There was no need to yell.

Finding the doctor was underwhelming.

After all the travel and rush and fast pace walking, Scott didn't catch Brayden, he happened upon the scientist by the side of the road.

Doctor Brayden was sitting there as if it took all his energy to stay seated up against that tree.

He lifted his head at the call of his name and Scott saw the only reason his head didn't fall all the way forward was because his neck was so swollen.

"Don't ..." Josh said. "Don't come any closer. I'm infected."

"I know and I'm pretty sure my clock is ticking down until I get it," replied Scott, stepping closer. "What are you doing?"

"I wanted to see my wife," Josh said in a whimpering manner. "I just wanted to see my wife."

"You know I can't let you do that. I can't let you near their camp."

"Is that why you're here? Following me and protecting my wife?"

"I am actually protecting my son. When you made the comment early on about sending your loved ones away, I sent my son here. I figured you'd know the safest place."

"It is."

"It's not if you're here. Or me for that matter."

"Maybe you won't get it."

Scott shrugged. "I can't assume that. I will ask you how long until I know I'm safe, if I'm safe."

"Ten days from last exposure is the longest I have seen in animals."

Scott nodded. "Yeah, well, I'm not counting on that. And I'm not counting on you getting close either." He pulled out his revolver. "I can't have you here. Can you walk?"

"Where are we going?"

"Away from as many people as we can."

"And then?" asked Josh.

"I can end it or wait until you die."

"I need to speak to my wife. It's so important, I have to tell her something. I have to. I can't die without letting her know things. If I can just get within distance of her hearing my voice."

"What do you have to tell her?" Scott asked. "I'm sure she knows you love her."

"It's not that." He weakly shook his head. "I need to tell her that I did this."

"We all know you created YPP-234."

"No, I did it. The accidental release. It's my fault."

His words didn't shock Scott, in fact Scott felt relief that not only wasn't it an act of war, but that he was right in his first guess.

"You're not surprised?"

General Scott shook his head. "Not at all. You were trying to sell the weapon before. Was this part of that?"

Josh nodded slowly. "It wasn't supposed to be a massacre. It was ... it was supposed to be a team, a hostage situation, we had the codes, there was no need to do what they did. The man who took it didn't follow my instructions."

"You didn't sell before, not because the price wasn't high enough, but because they couldn't do it safely. But you changed your mind. I would like to know why. What made you do this? What made you take your monster and sell it?"

"It's not greed," Josh wept. "Maybe it was. I just saw we couldn't heal after our son died. We couldn't bounce back."

"No amount of money in the world will heal that, trust me I know."

"I know too, but I was losing my wife. I thought since I was already losing my self-worth and reputation, take the money and take her away for good."

"Now the world is paying. What sucks is your Karma isn't getting it, it would have been you having to watch this happen and live with that. You have an easy way out, Doctor. Why the hearings? Why go to the Senator?"

"Because I changed my mind. I wanted to stop it," Josh explained. "I told the backers it was a cover for what was going to happen, but I wanted the sale to be stopped."

"Then you should have been honest. We could have secured the lab."

Josh began to get breathless. "I don't have much time. I really need to talk to Jen."

After a beat, Scott pulled out his phone. "I will tell my son to give the phone to your wife. But you will not deliver that news to her. She doesn't need to carry the guilt that comes with your confession." He began to dial the phone. "Don't do that to her."

Slowly, Josh nodded.

General Scott stared at him when Monty answered. "Yeah, I did. I found him. Monty, he wants to speak to his wife. Can you give her the phone? Thank you."

"Hello." Jen said softly. "Is this Monty's dad?"

"It is. Ma'am your husband isn't well. You understand for my son's sake and yours I cannot let him near your camp."

"I do," Jen replied.

"He would like to speak to you. We can give him that." General Scott handed the Sat phone to Josh.

He could barely take the phone, and it took everything he had to hold it to his ear. "Jen," Josh wept out. "Jen, I'm sorry. I love you. Everything I have done was for you and Matt. Please know that." He released a single sob. "Promise me you'll wait until this burns out. Don't leave. Six weeks. Eight if you can. It'll burn out fast." He paused. "Me, too. Yeah." He sniffled. "Don't give up. Matt wouldn't want that. I love you, too." He closed his eyes and his arm lowered. Josh glanced over fumbling to end the call and he pushed the phone aside.

General Scott reached for it.

"Don't," said Josh. "Don't touch the phone for four days. If you're still alive. Just don't touch that please." With what was left of his strength he pushed the phone aside. He then rolled slowly to his side and using his hands and knees, along with the tree, brought himself to a stand. He exhaled. "I'm ready. Let's get me farther away."

General Scott didn't say anything more. He just nodded his agreement, kept his distance and slowly led Josh into the woods.

He put his gun away, he wouldn't need it and wouldn't have to do a thing. Scott wasn't a doctor, but he could tell they probably wouldn't make it too far into the woods before the doctor of death joined all those who he was responsible for killing.

NINETEEN – THUMP

Deke was shaking. He gripped his phone so tight trying with everything he had to get in touch with his mother. She wasn't answering. No one was. It was surreal and he felt like he was smack dab in the middle of a video game. Sirens outside the apartment building, helicopters whirling overhead, shouting, people crying.

When did it all fall apart?

He went into panic mode when his mother first told him she had caught whatever his stepfather had.

"What do we do?" he asked Bebe. "What do we do?"

"We stay calm, stay inside and wait it out."

But it moved so fast.

From a plane on a runaway to the authorities saying to stay inside and report illness.

Everything crumbled.

He couldn't reach his father, his mother or his stepfather.

But he was safe with his stepmother, sister Ginny and little brother Dennis.

No matter what was going on outside, in the apartment they were safe.

Until they weren't.

Within hours Bebe said to him, "Baby, I'm sick. So is Dennis. Take your sister and stay away."

What?

She was sick. At first Deke thought she was overreacting. Mistaking symptoms of a cold for the sickness that was all over the news.

After all, none of them had left the apartment.

Then again, his stepfather and mother were both sick. They were at the apartment before they showed any illness.

She wouldn't come near Deke. He took his one year old sister into the back bedroom, then following his stepmother's instructions as she called from another room, Deke hid their food supply.

Water was hidden underneath the dirty laundry, canned goods behind the shoes, crackers and cookies were in with the toys.

Not everything. But she wanted him to hide some stuff just in case.

In case of what?

Bebe would get better, so would his mother and stepfather.

They had to. No one was saying anything to Deke and after the warnings came from the government the internet was spotty.

He put in a search on social media and everyone claimed they had it. One person said they watched people just drop over and die.

That couldn't be true. Nothing did that. No illness killed everyone. It had to be some sort of rumor gone bad. Like when people say a celebrity died and they didn't.

One thing was true, the illness, or fear of it, barreled over the world and fourteen year old Deke was at a loss as what to do.

He stayed in the back bedroom with Ginny, trying to keep the one year old occupied was tough, picking things up off the floor so she didn't put them in her mouth when she crawled around and climbed. She hadn't started really walking yet, so she wasn't too mobile.

Still, she cried.

"Mama, mama."

"I want my mom, too." Deke held her. His eyes lifted to the ceiling when he heard a hard thump from the apartment above. It sounded like someone fell. He wondered if they just dropped over dead like social media said.

"Deke," Bebe called out from a distance. "Sweetie it's time. We have to go."

Her voice sounded rough and thick as if she struggled to talk.

Deke stood up from the floor, holding his hand out to Ginny. "Stay. Okay." Despite her starting to cry, Deke slipped out and walked towards the bedroom.

Bebe was at the end of the hall, near the living room holding Dennis. His legs dangled and his head rested on her shoulder. It was the first time all day he had actually seen her and she wasn't overreacting. He could see how sick they were.

His heart thumped then sunk when he saw how truly sick she looked.

"What are you doing?" she asked. "Please get back in."

"I can't let you go until I see you. Where are they taking you?"

She shook her head. "I don't know."

"How long will you be gone?"

"I don't know. Deke, sweetie, I know, I know this is a lot for you to handle. Please know I adore you and you're so strong."

"I'm not strong Bebe. I'm scared," he said.

"We all are. Now you don't leave. You don't let anyone in. If by some chance, because things are bad, people break in, you let them take what they can see. Alright?"

"That's why I hid the food huh?"

Bebe nodded. "There's been a lot of looting. I'll lock the door when I leave. I wish we could get you somewhere safer, but I don't want you two leaving. Not until this is over."

"Okay, when?" Deke asked.

"The news said weeks."

"But you'll be back, right?"

"I hope." She said weepy. "But if—"

"No. Bebe."

"Listen to me. If I am not back, go to your mom's house. It'll be better and leave a note for your father. Because I feel it in my heart he'll be back."

"So will you."

"My sweet boy, I hope so."

Deke took a step toward hem.

"No." she held up her hand. "Please don't."

"I want to say goodbye to Den and you. I want to hug him."

Bebe squeezed Dennis. "This is from your brother." She kissed the sick boy. "He loves you baby. Deke loves you."

It took everything Deke had not to cry. Staring at Bebe and Dennis so sick, while Ginny cried in the bedroom.

"We gotta go. They'll be down there."

"Bebe, wait," Deke called out. "I love you. "

Her mouth tensed up then her lips quivered. "Oh, my sweet boy. I love you with everything I am. I am so lucky to have you in my life, so proud of you. Know that, okay?"

Deke nodded.

"Now go. Take care of Ginny." Bebe turned, looked once more over her shoulder and then walked away.

It broke his heart when the door closed and he heard it lock. He hoped it would be over soon, that Bebe, Dennis, his mother and stepfather would go to this medical place and get well.

But a part of Deke knew and feared that wasn't going to happen.

Bebe had seen it all before, only it was a movie.

The lines of people waiting to board buses, workers in space suits calling out orders, speakers on top of the buses gave instructions.

Holding tight to Dennis, Bebe looked around and to her apartment where Deke stared out the window. She had to turn with her body because she couldn't move her head left to right. She waved sadly, balancing Dennis. Yes he was heavy, however, she didn't care. It was her child.

The apartment complex had scores of red brick buildings, they all looked the same, all four stories. Apartments that were affordable and most who lived there weren't rich or even lucky enough to be middle class.

When she looked around in the commotion it reminded her of the old photos she saw of Kay dry hanging laundry between buildings. Only it wasn't laundry, it was a call for help.

As instructed by authorities each one was to place a towel, sheet or something to mark infection in the home. Bebe couldn't spit a single apartment without something hanging from a window.

They were flags of desperation and sickness.

Bebe didn't even know if someone would come, it seemed everyone was coming down with the illness from the weapon.

The news did break that there was an accident in a lab. They never really said it was a weapon, she found that out from Tammy and Daryl.

Now days later, everywhere was hit.

So why didn't they let Ellis go?

Probably the same reason they were gathering people to 'medical centers'. Keep the sick from the healthy, try to control and contain it.

When the news was released and they requested people to mark their homes, Bebe didn't know how that would work. They asked people not to go to the hospital because they were already overrun and provisions were being set up elsewhere to give treatment.

Treatment was a promising word.

She hung the towel out of the kitchen window the day before and in the morning, someone drove by using a loud speaker announcing that a transport would arrive at seven PM and for those that were not sick, to stay indoors during the transition.

"It is imperative," the man said over the speaker. "If you are sick to come get medical attention immediately."

So there she was, standing there, holding her child, standing in a long line.

Of course, every line to every bus was long. And the caravan of buses extended to the end of the block and beyond, there had to be at least a dozen. Then again, her apartment community was enormous.

Three times she made it near the entrance to the bus only to be told it was filled.

"It's okay baby," she told Dennis. "We'll be sitting down soon."

She hoped.

Bebe had never felt so sick in her life. Her whole entire body ached, she was fevered and her neck was so swollen she feared she would choke, because it felt like something was strangling her.

Finally, she decided to walk all the way to the end and at the last bus, there was no line. She could see a few people on there, whether they were from her community of Rolling Hills or were on there prior, she didn't know.

No one told her it was filled and relieved she and Dennis, stepped inside.

She was about to take the first row when she heard the call of her name.

"Bebe? Bebe?"

Bebe looked back, standing from a seat in the middle of the bus was Tammy.

Tammy? Why was she on a bus? It didn't make sense.

Bebe walked toward her and when she saw Deke's mother, she looked as sick as Bebe felt.

"You too?" asked Bebe.

Tammy nodded. "Sit with me, please." She reached out her hand and placed it on Dennis' head when Bebe sat. "Oh, this poor baby. I'm so sorry."

"Me, too."

"How's Deke?" Tammy asked.

"He's fine. Ginny, too."

Tammy gasped out. "Oh, thank God."

"The moment I started feeling sick, I kept him away. Dennis got sick really fast and when I saw Ginny wasn't, Deke took her."

"Maybe they'll be fine," Tammy said. "God, I pray they will."

Bebe spoke whimpering some. "I hate the thought of a fourteen year old boy having so much responsibility in such a horrible situation. He's alone, Tammy. I'm sorry. I'm so sorry."

"No, he'll handle it. Maybe ... maybe Ellis is fine and will get home."

"I hope so." Bebe took a deep breath. "Oh my God. Where's Daryl?"

At that instance, Tammy let out a single sob.'

"No," Bebe said in shock. "When?"

"This afternoon. It's still not real. That's how I ended up on this bus. We were on our way to one of the centers. His cousin let us know where one was. That was yesterday. We got stuck in traffic almost the whole day. My phone died, I didn't have my charger." She started crying. "And he died, Bebe. He died in the car. He said he couldn't breathe, and he died. His last words."

"Tammy, I am sorry."

"I got out of the car, you know. I'm screaming for someone to help me. Please, help me. No one did. Then I hated leaving him, but I am so sick. I was walking and the bus picked me up."

"I'm glad." Bebe grabbed her hand. "I'm glad you're here with me. We're together. We'll get through this."

Tammy gripped her hand. "We'll get through this, together."

And as the bus slowly rolled away from the affordable housing apartment community, Bebe turned some to look out the window just like Tammy. And probably, just like Tammy did so knowing she was watching the last of the world, her world as it fell apart.

<><><><>

Doctor Josh Brayden was dead.

A little before eleven PM, under the most beautiful, clear, star filled sky, the doctor died a horrendous death.

General Scott was never far from him, watching at a distance of twenty-feet. Not that it mattered. The young woman Katie was that same distance and still became the weapon that would cascade nothing but heartache to the world.

He actually carried on a conversation with Josh until the doctor could no longer speak louder than a whisper.

He asked how many people would this weapon kill when it

was all said and done.

Josh told him he feared the weapon and it was an answer he didn't know. It would burn out, but only two weeks after the last person fell ill.

Scott built a small fire and felt bad for Josh, he shouldn't have, but he did.

Then when Josh went into the final phase of the sickness it was nothing Scott would want to see happen to his worst enemy, even someone who inadvertently caused the end of the world.

It was a painful deal, delivering havoc on the body.

Josh shook, arms reaching out as he struggled to breathe, gasping out, "Help me. Help me."

Then the human being inside of Scott took over and he walked to the dying man, helping him sit up, grabbing his hand.

A part of him felt pity, another part felt it was justice.

Gasping. Choking. Crying.

"I didn't mean for this to happen," Josh said through struggling word. "I didn't mean it. I'm sorry. I'm sorry."

Death.

Without a gasping final breath, Josh just died.

General Scott was once again exposed.

Knowing that, he sought out his sat phone and called his son.

The battery was almost dead and he had one more call to make. A short one.

"I'm here. He's dead," said Scott. "Stay put. I'll be in the woods for two weeks, then if ... if I am alive and well, I will find you."

Monty was worried. But Scott assured his son he could live on the land. Though Monty conveyed he didn't doubt that, he still told Scott where he'd leave provisions in case he needed them.

One hundred percent certain he wouldn't last the week, Scott thanked his son, told him he loved him and ended the call.

If ... if he were to survive and not get sick, he had to last two weeks. Adding a couple days to the ten day time frame.

Two weeks.

His clock had started. It was only a matter of would he be alive when it was times up.

PART FOUR

SURVIVORS

TWENTY – THE IN BETWEEN

JFK QZ – New York

When Ossie was thirteen years old, many decades before, she started volunteering. It was her way to give back. It was her entire life. When someone needed something, she stepped up to the plate.

No worries, Ossie will lend a hand.

Ossie, can you help out.

Thank goodness you were there, Ossie.

Always. Even if she had to tote her two children around, she was there.

Up until the hangar.

In a snap of a finger, everything changed.

She was giving to Ellis on the plane and even for the first several days in the hangar.

Then her Rosalie got sick and became a turn of the page for a different Ossie.

Going on twelve days since they stepped into that quarantine hangar, Ossie was a shell of her former self.

She watched the last of her precious babies take their final breath as she held them in her arms, unable to take away the pain they were having. Holding back the need to scream because watching them suffer was torture, even though they were the ones feeling it.

Ossie watched as nearly everyone got sick, all but a handful of people, including Ellis.

Workers stopped coming in, the only reason there was still food was because so many were sick no one ate.

The young woman, the one from first class who was placed in a plastic cell. Ossie knew she carried the illness, delivering it to everyone.

She died.

But it wasn't from illness, more than likely dehydration. At first the workers dwindled from five to two, then none. When that happened they stopped bringing her food and water, and that was four days earlier.

Ossie never heard the young woman ask for water or anything else for that matter. Not that she would have given it to her. Ossie no longer bothered to ask Ellis if he needed anything or even worried about it.

Like the few others who survived, she was imprisoned in an electronic, cold death pit.

It didn't bother Ossie.

She stopped talking and she stopped caring. After wrapping her babies tightly in blankets, Ossie never left the area that was horribly deemed their final resting place. She sat on the floor, praying to God for the sickness take her. It was her turn, it was her time.

<><><><>

Holly River, WV

The fishing was good. On any given day, Scott, if he went early enough, would catch his meal. He had no problems living off the land, then again, he had only been doing it for four days. By nightfall it would be twelve days since the plane landed, five full days since Doctor Brayden died.

Scott had another week to wait.

Once and a while he'd see his son across the water, that was always Scott's sign to leave, he just didn't want to take any chances.

The next couple days were crucial, most people got sick two to five days after exposure.

On this day, he didn't see Monty, he heard him.

"Dad!"

At first he worried something was wrong, then his son, shouted.

"Don't run off. I left you a box!"

Scott smiled and hollered back. "Where?"

"It's a little jaunt, but not like you have anything to do. A mile down river, where it narrows, you'll see it on the walking bridge."

"Thank you!"

"No problem!" Monty yelled. "Are you okay?"

"Knock on wood. Yes. Are you guys?"

"Fine. Well, Jen is pretty down."

"That's to be expected!"

"What?"

Scott shook his head. "Nothing. Thank you, again."

"Countdown is on, Dad."

"I know. Good catching today, Monty."

"You, too."

"I'm done. I have a box to catch."

"What?"

Scott tossed his hands upward with a shake of his head. "I'll see you soon!" He gathered his items and left. He was lucky enough to find that old fishing rod. He had to make his own lures, but it helped pass the time.

He could have done with more drinking water. He was able to get some from the streams and created a filter.

No doubt he wasn't getting enough to eat, but enough to sustain himself.

He followed Monty's directions, walking by the edge of the water. He didn't spot a bridge for a while. It was a lot farther than a mile . But soon enough, there was a small rope bridge that crossed the narrow portion of the river.

He picked up his pace when he saw the bridge and the box was on his side of it.

It was a good size box, heavy, too. When he opened the flaps, on top was a note.

Dad,

I know you can handle this 'man of the land survivor guy stuff'', but let me help you for once. If you're smart and not me, this will last you. Love you. Be safe. M.

Scott really smiled when he read that note. He brought it to his lips, then folded it, placing it in his pocket. Inside were eight bottles of water, and rationing or not, Scott grabbed one right away and twisted off the cap. It tasted so good, but he had to control himself. Make the good stuff last.

There was some food in there, jerky, dried fruit, protein bars and chocolate chip cookies. A thermos was in there, and as he lifted it, thinking, 'wow, cold or not, I get coffee', he saw the instant coffee packets from the MRE's.

"What the heck?" He wondered what was in the small thermos and opened, he didn't even need to look, he caught the smell of whiskey right away. He'd ration that as well.

Reorganizing the box that he rummaged through, Scott would take it back to his campsite.

He lifted it with gratefulness. Not because of the items, but more so because his son put it there. His son was safe. Scott couldn't imagine what it would be like to have a child alone out there in a plague ravaged world, especially a young child.

Sadly and undoubtedly there were many children out there, alive and alone fending for themselves.

<><><><>

Baldwin, PA

It was one of those hot fall days. Too warm during the day and Deke opened the window in hopes to get a breeze inside the stuffy apartment. He'd leave it open just a short time, enough to maybe cool things down. He knew Bebe was neurotic about that window and was always scared Ginny would try to climb out. He glanced out the window. The complex, which was large with walkways and paths always had people walking about or driving on them. Now everything is empty with the exception of a few people running across the grassy areas carrying things.

The sirens in the distance had stopped, as did the choppers and gun fire.

It was quiet.

Scary. He hoped he didn't have to worry about what he and Ginny would do next, where they would go.

Maybe Bebe would be back.

He hadn't heard from her since Bebe called him from the bus and put his mother on the phone. They were all going to the emergency medical camp together. That was a good thing. But then he didn't hear back and the phones stopped working.

He thought about his father, was he ill? Was he alright? But his main focus was on Ginny.

He kept her fed, her diaper changed, and most importantly, he kept her quiet. He had to. When he started speaking in whispers, his baby sister mimicked.

Deke never thought they'd have to be quiet, but three times people knocked on their door, sometimes hard, asking for food. Deke didn't answer. Once, the man sounded so hostile, pounding to get in, Deke covered Ginny's mouth until he went away.

It was scary, it really was. Especially since the power went down. He wasn't a hero or brave, he was just a teenager, still trying to figure things out. He was tasked with not only watching, but protecting, his one year old sister. The nights were the worst. A dim apartment lit by one flashlight or candle. Deke would be too scared something would happen and fought to stay awake until he just passed out.

If an outsider were to observe the situation they would wonder how Deke did it. The days moved slowly, the hours crept by. He slept when she did, waiting for Bebe to get back or when they'd have to leave.

He feared that.

His baby sister didn't know much. She didn't speak other than babble one or two words. She didn't walk or know how to use the bathroom. The diapers were dwindling, and Deke was spending his free time going through his parents' old clothes trying to make diapers.

"I know, I know," Deke said. "It's lunch. You're hungry." He filled her sippy cup with half a juice box to try to appease her. He rationed what they had in the kitchen and living room, not touching their hidden stash until he had to.

He fixed them a lunch of crackers and soup. The stove still worked even though the lights had gone out the day before.

"Here you go," he told her.

Bang!

The hard slam against the apartment door caused his heart to skip a beat and a shock wave jolted through his body.

Ginny looked to where the sound came from.

Bang. Bang.

Someone wasn't knocking at the door, they were slamming into it trying to get in.

He wanted to scream, "Go away!" But he was scared to make a noise. He grabbed Ginny and her sippy cup, along with her small bowl and hoisted her into his arms.

Again there was a bang at the door, only this time he could hear the frame crack.

Deke didn't know what to do. The only thing he could think of was to protect his sister.

Run to the back bedroom, lock the door and hide. That was his thought.

Whoever was trying to get in didn't want Deke or the baby, they couldn't. After all, Deke didn't do anything.

With Ginny in his arms, he bolted toward the back bedroom. The moment he set her down inside the room, he realized he dropped her sippy cup somewhere in that short run. If he wanted to hide, to keep her quiet, he needed it.

"Stay," he told her then raced back for it.

What was he thinking?

He saw it. It was just at the end of the hall near the living room.

Grab it he thought, and run back.

Just as his fingers touched upon it, a loud crack rang out as the door to the apartment burst open.

"I told you someone was in here," a man said. "Just grab what they have."

Deke grabbed the half-filled sippy cup, lifted it and before he could turn. He saw one of the men.

"Where's the food?" the man blasted.

"Just don't hurt us," Deke pleaded.

"Where's the food?"

"In the kitchen."

"Should have answered the door."

Then as if Deke was a full grown person, the man, grabbed him, lifted him by the shirt and hit him with a closed fist. Deke felt his entire body go limp.

The man dropped Deke to the ground, and Deke felt the sippy cup topple from his grip. As he reached for it, the man laughed, as if it were some sadistic game to him.

Taking his frustration out on Deke, that had to be what it was. He stomped Deke's hand then kicked him in the gut.

Deke had never felt anything like that before. Every bit of air oozed from his body and he gasped for breath as his stomach knotted.

He tried to crawl away, but the man kicked him again.

"Leave him alone. Just grab what we need," another shouted.

In that hallway, Deke rolled over slowly, thinking he was safe and when he did, all he saw was a shoe coming down at his face.

It connected.

Deke never felt the pain of that curb stomp, he was out cold.

A searing burning pain shot through Deke's entire torso, worsening with even the slightest movement.

The pain.

That was all Deke registered a second after he felt the cool air against his face. That was fleeting and replaced with pure, unadulterated panic when he opened his eyes and saw it was dark.

He didn't care that he was hurt, a flood of fear and panic took over him immediately.

Ginny.

He had been knocked out long enough for it to get dark. Deke stood without regard to the pain, freaking out internally even more when he realized how quiet it was.

"Ginny." He called out her name.

No response. Deke had to find her. It was too dark to see anything. As he made his way to the kitchen for the flashlight, he felt air again through that window and feared she may have crawled out like Bebe always worried about. What if the men who beat him and robbed the apartment did something to her?

What if they had killed her?

If that didn't happen, numerous other things could have. Ginny could have choked, fallen, crawled from the apartment.

"Ginny!" Deke screamed, his chest was heavy and his throat tightened as he fought back crying and sobbing.

How could this happen?

It was his baby sister. He was supposed to be responsible for her.

"Please, please, please answer me. Please be alright." Deke swung that light around the living room, she wasn't there. He didn't want to look out the window, he was too scared. "Ginny, please." He sobbed once as he walked down the hall.

It was scary for him to look in the bathroom, she could have fallen in there or got in the toilet.

She was only a baby, she didn't know any better. She had to be so scared. Deke was supposed to watch her, protect her.

He wanted to die, just crumble and die. Where was his sister?

At the end of the hall he reached the door to the back bedroom, the one they spent a lot of time in. He remembered putting her in there and closing the door.

But did he lock it? Was it closed all the way?

Taking a deep breath, holding his side, he aimed the flashlight in the room. As soon as he did, he saw Ginny on the floor. She lay on her side, blanket by her, gold fish crackers spread about and that sippy cup was in her hand.

"Please be alive. Please be alive." Deke rushed to her and dropped down to the floor. He placed his trembling hand on her back. When he touched her, she inhaled and sighed in her sleep.

Hearing her breathe, Deke, exhaled a sob and lay next to her, cradling the baby. "I'm so sorry." He kissed her. "I'm so sorry."

Thinking about what she saw, what she did, how she was so alone, even though it wasn't his fault, it still made him feel horrible.

He was so appreciative that she was alive, he vowed he would never let her out of his sight again. Deke felt scared and alone, like a lost child. Because in so many ways he was still a child.

He wanted his father, his mother, Bebe, someone.

Deke needed help and no one was there.

In pain and probably still bleeding, Deke stayed right next to Ginny and silently wept.

TWENTY-ONE – THE FEW

JFK QZ – New York

A man named Garret was in his mid-forties and he, along with Ellis and a woman named Joan, were the only remaining survivors that weren't with family on the plane.

The others like Ossie watched their children, spouse, grandchildren ... die.

Maybe that was why they could move the dead from the CDC and army trailers. Once the guards died and the workers stopped coming in the hangar, Ellis walked outside for fresh air.

He realized after the first breath of autumn air that the hangar was even more horrendous smelling than he realized inside.

The smell was all over his clothes.

He found the first mobile lab and some clothes in there. He used the disinfectant shower to get clean, even though he knew he'd have to clean up again and again.

He and Garret started lining up the bodies in a dignified way while Joan tried to find identification on them. They had none from the hangar, not yet.

They didn't immediately start clearing the dead, it took a day or two to get to that point. What else were they going to do?

They started at sun up on this day and already were getting tired, and it wasn't even noon.

Garret wiped the sweat from his brow. "I think it's time."

Ellis looked at his watch. "Yeah, it is." He shook his head and walked toward the fence. Near there were a pile of shoes and he picked one up tossing it at the fence. It sizzled and popped. Hands on hips he returned to where Garret and Joan stood.

Joan sighed out disapprovingly. "I keep telling you that fence will remain on until there's no power."

"Which is a good sign," Garret said. "The moment it goes down, that means no one is manning stations. We're not on generators here. It's connected somehow to the airport."

"It's just frustrating, you know," Ellis said. "I need to go home."

"We're doing our part here," replied Joan. "As long as we are here, our families are safe from whatever this is. We have to believe that. They're just waiting for us all to die out."

"You would think someone would come for the workers," Ellis stated. "I mean, the military, CDC. Someone should come."

Garret shook his head. "I'm not a doctor, I just watch a lot of these types of movies and this is bad. I mean, all these people that are dead are wearing protective suits and they still got it."

"How are we still alive?" asked Ellis.

"We have some sort of immunity or resistance. Unlike these poor souls."

Joan lifted her hand. "Okay, worst case scenario. No one comes. Power goes down. Do we bury these people or just leave?"

"I say," Garret replied. "We go for an old-fashioned Viking funeral. It's respectful."

"You mean burn them?" Ellis cringed.

"It's better than walking away, and I don't know about you but I have a family up north I need to find. It would take weeks to bury everyone."

"Speaking of burying everyone." Ellis looked at the hangar. "I'm gonna go check on Ossie before going into that last CDC mobile. That's the last one so maybe there is some information in there."

"One of them has to have something," said Garret.

"You would think. I'll let you know." Ellis nodded then

walked toward the hangar, grabbing a bottle of water from their rations table.

The plastic still hung over the hangar, a vain attempt to keep the bug in, obviously it didn't work. Ellis could smell death before he was ten feet from the door, it was overwhelming.

Before stepping in he placed on one of those paper masks, not for protection, but to block some of the odor. He had doused it with lemon scented disinfectant spray. It didn't completely work, but it helped.

Ossie was in the same spot he saw her hours before. Sitting on the floor, a blanket over her.

Ellis felt so bad for her, she definitely was a shell of the woman that was on the plane from London.

"Hey," he spoke softly, approaching Ossie with an extended bottle of water. "Here. Please. Drink this."

She shook her head.

"Ossie, I know it's bad, okay? I do. But you have a son and daughter beyond that fence. They still need you."

"Oh, Ellis. You are a parent. Your heart tells you and your gut confirms. My children are no longer with us."

"No." Ellis shook his head. "That's not true. Beyond that fence is normalcy."

"If you feel like that, then your family is fine."

"So is yours. And when that fence is off, I will personally help you bury your grandchildren. But I need you strong. I need you to drink this."

She finally relented and took the bottle.

"That fence will come down," said Ellis. "It'll give you hope."

Ossie didn't reply to him and Ellis was fine with that. There was very little he could do for her, but he would try.

He made his way out of the hangar and to the final CDC mobile lab. It was at that moment, when he stepped in, every cliché about the best being last came true.

The smell of rotting flesh pelted him the second he opened the door. And he was only in the front portion. Most of the mobile labs were broken into three rooms. A small entrance room, usually with a desk. The second was a lab, but not one where they worked on the viruses, the third portion was for that. To get in and out of the lab, a person had to enter through the back by way of the disinfectant chamber and biohazard suit, dressing room.

That first small room was void of people or bodies, but the door was slightly ajar. Ellis knew that was where the smell came from.

Sure enough it was. Bingo! On the couch, laying there covered in a blanket was a woman and decomposing or not, he knew it was Senator Lenore James. Across from her, seated in a chair was another body. A woman with short gray hair, she was slumped over in a chair, the mouse to the computer still in her hand. She worked until her last dying breath.

There were four monitors on the counter desk. The far left screen had science looking stuff, cells, viruses, Ellis guessed. The middle two were camera angles of the entire hangar and what looked like the labs and disinfectant chambers. There wasn't an image or camera angle that didn't have bodies or death.

The fourth monitor looked more like a word document, it shared the screen with some sort of inter-office messenger.

The last two messages were two days earlier.

"Anything?" Was marked by the name RebO.

With the reply from T-Bon of '*Working. We'll get back.*'

From the colors of the messages, he figured RebO was the woman.

"Thank you for trying so hard," Ellis said to her. "I'm sorry this happened to you."

All on that counter were papers. Maybe, just maybe there were answers and notes.

Something.

He lifted the stack and started going through them. Handwritten notes were on a clipboard, almost like a hourly diary.

His caught her last entry.

Waiting for T. Bonoski. He may be our best hope.

T. Bonoski. That had to be T-Bon on the messengers. He flipped through the pages, skimming for another reference.

Two pages, dated days earlier, his name was mentioned and a notation about University of Pittsburgh.

It was a sign to Ellis. He told Ossie he was going to find hope and sure enough it was in his home town, not to mention the last written word of a hardworking woman was the word 'hope'.

Ellis decided to share his findings with Ossie. He turned to leave but stopped when he heard the bling of the computer.

It caused Ellis to jump a little and he glanced down. His eyes widened.

T-Bon.

Ellis may have been a few feet away, but he could read the words.

'I may have it. Give me two hours, Bec, I'll know for sure.'

"Oh my God," Ellis ran to the computer and tried to reply, but he needed to move the cursor to the messenger window. It was floating somewhere.

The mouse was in the woman's hand. Thankfully he was wearing gloves, Ellis reached for her hand and pried the mouse from it. As he did, he watched the message close.

"No!" Ellis freaked for a second, then noticed he had only minimized it. He opened the app, placed the cursor and replied. *'Bec has passed away. Did you really find the cure? How are things outside this camp?"*

Ellis knew it was several questions, but he desperately needed the answers. He hit send and watched the messenger read, 'sending'.

It kept saying 'sending'.

Then it beeped.

Connection lost.

What horrible timing for the internet and lines to go down. But at least he knew, out there was hope, and he was going to show it to Ossie.

With the clipboard in hand, along with a file folder and loose papers, Ellis raced out of the mobile.

He headed to the hangar and bolted inside.

"Ossie. Ossie, I have ..."

She wasn't there. Her normal spot was empty. Where was she?

The bathroom maybe?

There were four other people in there alive and well.

"Anyone see Ossie?"

A mumbling voice replied softly. "She got up and walked out."

"Oh," Ellis said with surprise. "Thanks."

Did she finally decide to get some fresh air? Maybe his words had motivated her. It made him happy she went outside and Ellis went back out to find her.

He didn't see her. He spotted Garret by the ration table.

"Hey," Ellis called out. "Have you seen Ossie?"

"No." Garret shook his head and brought the bottle of water to his mouth. "Wait." He lowered the bottle and looked beyond Ellis. "What is she doing? Ellis," Garret said with slight panic. "What is she doing? Shit." He dropped the bottle and ran toward Ellis.

Ellis spun around. He saw Ossie. She was walking away and to his horror walking directly to the fence.

Dropping all those papers, Ellis ran for her, calling out. "Ossie! The fence is live! Stop!"

She didn't respond. She kept walking.

At that moment, Ellis started to run. He ran as fast as he could, heart racing, heaving out heavily. Death getting closer with each pounding footstep, but his legs wouldn't move fast enough.

She was too close to the fence, her arms outstretched.

He knew what she was doing.

"Ossie! No!"

Ellis heardGarret calling out as well for her to stop.

She didn't.

Every bit of his body shook. When Deke was three, he ran into the street, slipped from Ellis' hand as they came out of the store, and he took off. Top speed for the street. Ellis saw the car barreling down the road and he knew he couldn't reach his son. Had it not been for a stranger grabbing Deke, he would've witnessed the most horrific thing in his life.

But as he ran for Ossie he knew there would be no stranger intervening.

She wasn't stopping and Ellis, like that day in front of Schwartz's Market, knew he wasn't fast enough.

"No! Please. Ossie! No!"

Closer.

Closer.

"No!"

Ossie arrived at that fence, her hands touched it.

Ellis screamed and turned.

But nothing.

No snap, pop, sizzle.

The fence was dead.

Ellis dropped to his knees, instantly and emotionally drained. He gasped over and over between relief and tears, unable to move.

"I thought you tested that like fifteen minutes ago?" Garrett asked.

"I did." Ellis looked up.

Garret walked to Ossie.

She was standing at that fence, holding on to the links, shaking it, crying out. "No. Why don't you work? No!"

Garret reached her and tried to pull her away, but she wouldn't let go. Ellis finally stood, his legs rubbery as he staggered to Ossie.

He shook his head to Garret and whispered, "Let her go. I got this."

Garret nodded, laying a hand on Ellis' shoulder as he walked by. "That was so close."

"Ossie." Ellis walked to her.

Her head was against the fence as she sobbed.

"Ossie, I know you feel desperate."

"You don't know."

"I do. But the fence is down. That means we can leave. We can bury your family and look for your children. You're stronger than you think you are." He stepped closer. "I know those probably aren't the right words to say, I don't know what to say. I just know, for the sake of your children that are beyond this fence, you need to search for them. Just like I need to search for my family."

Slowly, Ossie, slid down, her fingers trailing over the metal fence as she dropped to the ground and leaned against it crying.

Ellis reached for her and she swatted him away.

"Okay." He raised his hands and stepped back. "Just know, I went to find you in that hangar because I promised you I'd find hope. Well, I found hope, find me if you want to know what it is." Ellis turned.

He didn't know how the fence suddenly went down, but by some miracle it was. As he walked away from her, he realized, the exterior lights were all out. The spotlights that were on twenty-four seven, were no longer on. The power was out.

Ellis didn't look at the bad side of no power, and maybe everything else had shut down. He didn't think of that scenario or wonder why. He just looked at it and thought it was his way to finally get home.

TWENTY-TWO – LITTLE TOO LATE

Pittsburgh, PA

He was the last one left and so was she.

Doctor and patient.

Unlike the others patients, he knew Anise's name. Just her first name, that was enough. Doctor Trent Bonoski was a professor at the University of Pittsburgh, He had taught biology, but remembered the days well when he worked on a super antibiotic for SARS. That was when he was younger, more energetic.

He was pulled in right away, not knowing what he was dealing with.

Trent was told it was a bacterium highly resistant to any antibiotics. When he reviewed it, it for sure looked like the plague.

He was told nothing about it and to figure it out on his own.

Everyone, everywhere was working on it.

They weren't kidding.

Nothing worked.

Not even the prototypes they had hidden away for when the next super bug arrived.

He went from working in a lab, to helping outside in the tents with patients.

But now his focus was on Anise. He thought about a nurse named Kay who worked up until she died. How she just told

Trent that it wasn't worth it. Why was he still trying?

His response was simple. He needed to find a cure because it wasn't over.

Maybe he would have given up had it not been for Anise.

She was his inspiration. How could she not be?

He thought back to four days earlier when she came to the medical camp. It was two days before Trent's eureka moment.

She arrived with the bulk of patients. The hordes of people that came in a wave seeking help. She wasn't randomly selected to be one of the twenty for test treatment. The prerequisite to be placed was each patient had to be in an earlier stage. She was in the third group to be tested. Tested with different antibiotics, combinations, or new ones

The University of Pittsburgh was a teaching hospital and a beacon in medical breakthroughs.

Maybe that was why so many people came to the medical camp there.

Hope against hope.

Trent hoped as well, there was so much to try.

But it wasn't going well.

Anise was different.

Trent didn't even know her name when he first met her. But now she was like his best and only friend.

While waiting on the final results, which he was positive would confirm what he knew. He sat in a chair next to Anise's bed reading the chart he had put together for her.

He was so meticulous in his notes because he never knew if he would get sick. Trent wanted someone to know the medical aspect of all that had happened.

His eyes glanced from the chart to Anise.

His initial notes stated she was a sixty-four year old African American woman, roughly five foot six, one hundred forty pounds and was exhibiting phase two, in his exact words, out of the four phases of bubonic plague.

Phases of plague.

When Trent saw that he thought it sounded like some soap

opera.

Stay tuned for the next installment of ... Phases of Plague.

Perhaps he was just tired or slap happy.

No medical personnel 'officially' called it stages or phases. Usually calling it stages were in essence of the three types of plague. But for his research and for future scientists, he documented a 'phase'

Trent's symptoms and progression phases were for the bubonic form. That was what he saw most of in regards to cases. Rarely was it pneumatic or septicemia. Those individuals with those two forms were usually dead within a day. They were even more aggressive.

Trent thought about how he worded it. Out of all the people they put in for test treatment, there were only nine real charts created.

Those nine individuals showed progress or what he called phases.

Inside each chart was a printed explanation of each phase.

Phase one of the bubonic form was the onset of symptoms. Headache, general malaise and disorientation. Phase two was pronounced swelling of lymph nodes and fever. Phase three was the appearance of fluid in the bulbous. Phase four was an extremely enlarged, fluid filled bulbous, which inhibited movement in the area. Death was imminent.

The time frame from phase one to three varied, but usually between phase three and death was no more than thirty-six hours.

The patient experienced insurmountable suffering and their post mortem state was simply a desecration of the human body.

However, Anise was different. Because of her incoherent rambling, Trent had that 'Yes! That could be it!" moment.

Slowly drifting into phase three, barely able to talk because her neck was approaching twice its normal size, a defiant Anise swatted Trent away and said, "You can't fight fire with fire."

Doctor Lowenstein's' fantasy project.

You can't fight fire with fire.

Or can you?

Doctor Allan Lowenstein was a brilliant scientist who insisted the future of healing was not just in synthetic antibiotics but synthetic antibiotics created for the individual illness. Utilizing new and well known synthetic antibiotics, the unique treatment was derived using isolated bacterium samples or cultures, all fed into his computer model with AI technology.

He was having amazing results with stubborn bacterium

Then the accident happened with NATO like something out of the Terminator movie, AI caused a conflict. Global nuclear war was narrowly avoided when it was learned there was no 'bad' country launching, it was bad choices for all superpowers to rely on AI.

After the intercepted nuclear bomb on its way to Moscow was detonated, a rapid response, and Trent believed ignorant initiative began, and within eight months AI was outlawed in science and military aspects.

Science was medical.

Lowenstein's project was officially shut down. But he, like probably many others kept going and used AI secretively.

When Anise said that, he made a beeline across campus to Lowenstein's lab. Trent knew where it was kept, what the program was hidden under and how to operate it.

He was one of Lowenstein's confidents. Trent fired up the system and ran the program. It was too fast and simple to be believable. Just as fast as he entered the data, the machine spit out the logical and best treatment for the sickness.

He merely had to take the data to the production machine and after two hours, he had the medication.

It was too easy. Trent didn't think there was any way it would work.

When he went back down to the testing field, the others he was going to give the medication to had progressed beyond the point of no return.

Not Anise, she was close though and Trent gave her the medication.

Within three hours not only did her fever break her neck swelling had decreased. He gave her another dose on schedule and sent a message to Rebecca Obadiah of the CDC.

If the medication worked, if Anise continued to progress positively, then Trent knew he was on to something.

There were others he gave it to and didn't get the same response. They could have been too far gone or Anise was an anomaly.

Whatever the case, he believed he saved at least one person. If he could save one, he could save more.

It was a waiting game.

He checked to see if Rebecca replied but saw her server lost power.

Trent couldn't dwell on that. He had to focus on Anise. To him it appeared she looked better with each passing moment.

It was unreal. Too simple. He and others spent countless hours reinventing the antibiotic wheel and nothing worked. But when he thought about it, the working solution made sense.

Fighting fire with fire was the key.

Trent had to fight synthetic with synthetic.

What better way to beat a souped up synthetic version of the Bubonic Plague than to use a souped up synthetic version of Gentamicin, the common antibiotic used to treat plague.

It was working. Whether or not it would cure Anise completely remained to be seen, but Trent was hopeful.

TWENTY-THREE – BREATHER

Holly River, WV

'Bacon makes everything better.' At least that was what Monty believed. He didn't have much of it and vowed to ration it, but he felt everyone needed something good to eat.

A treat,

When his father yelled across the water to ask if he could borrow Monty's car, he didn't hesitate to say yes. He took the car to a safe distance, just after sunup. Before he did so, he made bacon and eggs.

He took a plate to Jen, then left the food in his car for his father, eating his as he walked back.

When he arrived back at camp, he dropped off his empty plate and went over to Jen's.

She was sitting on the steps of her cabin and when Monty got closer, he saw the empty plate and smiled. "Oh, wow,' he said, "Cool, you ate."

"I was hungry. Thank you. Plus, you know, bacon."

Monty nodded and sat next to her. "Bacon makes everything better."

Her semi peaceful smile turned into a sad look and she stared.

"Maybe not everything," Monty said. "How are you doing?"

"Wishing I could have said a real goodbye to Josh. We were together nearly thirty years."

"My parents were together thirty as well."

"Divorced?" Jen asked.

"No. My mom died in a car accident," A lump formed in Monty's throat. "With my older brother."

"Oh, Monty, I'm sorry. When was this?"

"Three years ago. There's a lot to the story, I'll tell you one day."

"I'd like that. Any time you want to talk."

"I appreciate that," Monty said. "And I know how bad this is for you. But I'm here. And I'm sure your son is safe out there as well. I mean if Josh made you get safe, for sure he took care of his kid."

"That's something I kind of dance around." Jen glanced down to her hands. "Matthew died. When I met you, you looked so much like him, reminded me so much of him, that I ended up not wanting to tell you and make you feel weird."

"Dude, no, and I am sorry. That sucks and there are no words. I'm honored I can make you feel a little better."

"Monty." She reached over and grabbed his hand. "You have been a godsend. No pressure."

"No pressure."

"So, tell me, why bacon and eggs this morning?"

"My dad caught me at the lake. We had that cross water, yelling talk and he wanted my car. I took it to where he needed me to leave it and made him bacon."

"Because it makes everything better?" Jen asked with a slight smile.

"Yep. At least I think so."

"Where is he going?"

"Back to New York. He said he left those people in quarantine and needs to see if they are still there."

"Will he let them out?" Jen questioned.

"I guess. I don't know. I just feel a little nervous."

"About the people in quarantine or your dad being out there?"

"Neither." Monty shook his head. "About my dad taking my

car. I made bacon to help butter him up."

Jen chuckled. "Why? Is he that bad of a driver?"

"No. My car is that much of a mess. He's gonna freak."

"Oh, stop." Jen waved out her hand. "Things are falling apart in the world. A messy car is nothing."

"It's really, really, messy."

"Monty, really," she said. "How bad can it be?"

When General Scott arrived at his son's twelve year old Toyota he knew Monty had just been there. On the driver's seat of the car was a plastic container with bacon and eggs. Condensation was on the inside of the container and it was still semi warm. Before going anywhere or even getting in the driver's seat, Scott gobbled that breakfast and was so grateful for his son's thoughtfulness.

Then he got in the car.

For a split second he wondered if Monty actually made the breakfast or if it was leftover from some other time.

Scott made it from the side of the road and about ten feet when he stopped, put the car in park and got out with a frustrated and disgusted, "I can't. I just can't."

He should have known by the smell when he got in. It was bad.

Had his son not learned anything about tidiness from Scott? Had Scott not known Monty had lived with him his entire life, he would have sworn the boy lived in his car ... for years.

He could not conceivably travel eight hours in that car. No way. The neat freak in him would have an anxiety attack. He searched the car for something to collect the garbage and it disgusted him even more.

In the trunk there was a black garbage bag, but it was full and soft. It didn't feel like garbage. Perhaps a Goodwill donation bag or something. Not that he even knew Monty to do that, but Scott had. When Scott opened it to see if he could empty it a blast of dirty laundry odor and socks blasted his way.

With a grunt and ugh he took a second. "Are you kidding me? Why the hell do you have dirty laundry in the car?" And then his memory answered that question.

At least a month ago, he had told Monty he needed to do his own laundry, it was piling up and Monty said he'd go to the laundromat. Apparently, he never did. Hating to do it, but Scott needed that bag, he decided to dump those clothes in the trunk. Holding his breath he dumped the bag and reached for the trunk. Before closing it he got irritated again when he saw those PT shorts he had been looking for.

With the bag in hand, he proceeded to empty the garbage from the car. Soda cans, empty energy drinks and too many smashed fast food bags to count littered the car. And socks? Why were there socks, not to mention the thirty crushed empty packs of cigarettes?

Thirty.

Scott counted.

After a needed but annoying twenty minute delay, the car was tolerable enough to drive and Scott was on his way. He'd worry about the dirty dash and foggy looking windshield later. He knew he could make it to New York by evening and get to those left in quarantine. Scott felt guilty about leaving them locked up and behind. He knew there were plenty of provisions. He had to let them out, if any of them remained.

<><><>

JFK – New York

Ellis kept his promise, not because he had to, but because he wanted to and really there was no other choice.

He buried Ossie's family.

Before looking for a place to dig, which wasn't easy considering they were surrounded by concrete, they had to know if there was another option.

Perhaps getting help, calling the authorities. The moment

they knew for certain those electronic fences were down, Ellis found a car in the QZ zone and decided to drive out.

Look for that help.

He drove off the runaway and didn't have to go far to know, things at least in New York were bad.

He was trying to find his way to the road, there always was an entrance near the cargo hangars. And he did. But he didn't need to even take that road.

Six minutes passed and not a single car drove by. It wasn't a back road either, there were businesses he could see across the street, a fast food place for one.

Nothing.

No one.

Ellis turned back, but not before finding a place that had dirt and an area to dig a grave.

After he and Garret dug the graves, they placed Ossie's deceased family in the car and took them there.

It was the least he could do.

The sun was starting to set when they finally finished. Joan suggested they take a ride over the runways to the main terminal. See if there was power, see if there was help.

Ossie just wanted to get to her house, see if her children were alive or dead.

It became quickly apparent there wasn't any power anywhere and the overcast sky blocked out any stars and light from the moon.

It was completely black, and because traveling would be dangerous, they stayed inside the fast food place.

Garret broke into the back door, no one was there and it was good to be inside somewhere without bodies.

Because the power hadn't been out too long, the freezer items were still cold and they had food.

By morning, the sun barely up in the sky, Joan and Garret had found a car and were ready to head north to Connecticut where they both lived.

Ellis hated to separate; they were such a small group. No one wanted to stick together. The other four who had survived the QZ zone didn't hesitate to leave. There were plenty of military vehicles and cars.

But Ellis understood, he himself wanted to find his family.

He would do so after he took Ossie home. It was sort of on his way home, just a small detour. It wasn't even a question of whether to do so or not. Ellis wasn't a selfish person and abandoning others just wasn't like him. He wasn't about to abandon Ossie, hopefully, for her sake, her family was alive and well, just like Ellis believed his to be.

TWENTY-FOUR – HEALING

Baldwin, PA

Ginny knew three, one syllable words. Simple words. Ma, Da, and Boo.

Sitting on the floor, her sippy cup wedged in her hand, she pointed to Deke's face.

"Boo," she said.

"Yeah, Gin-Gin," Deke repealed weakly. "Deke got a boo-boo."

Boo-Boo was an understatement.

Deke was hurt badly. It hurt to breathe, to move or to cough. Not to mention his face just stung with every facial expression he made.

After being pulverized a couple days earlier, Deke had barely moved. He used most of his strength right after he came to, to create a blockade on the front door. He found a kitchen knife and bat to use as weapons. All their food and water remaining were brought to the back bedroom and that was where Deke stayed with Ginny.

He had to keep her safe, but he wasn't sure he could. He wasn't even able to do it when he wasn't injured.

Deke moved as little as he could, but he also knew laying down wasn't good for his breathing. Thankfully he did have Ginny to watch, to feed and take care of. She was his focus.

That and thinking about what to do next. They couldn't stay in the apartment forever.

He wasn't worried about those men who came into the apartment. Since it happened they hadn't come back. Probably because they took everything in the kitchen and fridge. Plus the flashlight and any medicine that was in the house.

Deke had no ibuprofen or even a band aid.

His first instinct was to leave, to wait for another bus with the baby to one of those medical camps or wherever they took Bebe and his brother.

He listened for the buses again.

No more ever came.

In fact, each day, each hour that passed grew increasingly quiet.

Bebe's car was still outside, Deke could see it, her keys were on the dresser in her room. Not that he knew how to drive, but he was sure he could figure it out. He knew the basics, so driving was an option. Walking was also an option, but did he have the strength to carry Ginny? Deke thought about that backpack, baby carrier, putting her in there and taking off, but that was bound to be heavy. Bottom line was Deke was useless until he healed a little. As long as he could provide Ginny with what she needed right now, they'd be fine.

The biggest worry he had was if different looters came in.

They were done for if that happened.

He thought a lot about his mother, brother, Bebe and his dad. Were they okay? Maybe they would be back before Deke was well enough to leave.

After all it was a flu of sorts, how long would they really be sick for?

They could walk in at any moment.

That was a fantasy, someone coming to his rescue. However, he was smart enough to know he couldn't count on anyone saving them.

It was up to Deke.

A scary reality was because of the looters, their food was running really low, so was the water. Maybe a day or two tops, then Deke wouldn't have a choice but to leave.

He'd figure it out, he would. But until he had to leave, Deke was trying his hardest to get better for his sister.

<><><><>

Trent placed his hands over Anise's as he passed her a mug of tea.

"You got it? Are you good?" he asked.

"I'm fine. I'm strong enough to hold a cup of tea," she said bringing it to her lips.

"Wish it could be more than store brand."

"Oh, honey, I can drink any brand. Except that flower stuff. No way." She shook her head. "This is going to be delicious because you made it for me."

Trent smiled. Anise was better. Not one hundred percent, but getting there.

He had moved her to the soft leather couch in one of the offices to finish her rest. Much better than the cot style bed.

It was a miracle.

One moment she was healing slowly and the next she was trying to walk to the bathroom.

"How are you feeling?" Trent asked.

"Much better. I feel better than when I came in." She sipped her tea.

"The treatment worked. Because of something you said I was able to find a cure that worked."

"I can't imagine what it was, I don't remember much after I came in."

"Just know I couldn't have done it without you. I am so happy you're on the mend. You're a strong woman."

"That I am, but I'm also a wise woman. And I know I'm not so special that I get my own private doctor. Things are bad, aren't they?"

Trent nodded.

After another sip, Anise extended the cup to the table. Trent took it and set it down.

"Be straight with me," she said. "I watched my husband, daughter and granddaughter die before we even made it inside here. There were thousands out there. How many died?"

"Might be easier to ask how many survived."

"How many?" She asked.

Trent held up a single finger.

"Oh sweet Lord," she gasped. "No."

"Yeah and fast, too."

"That explains my personalized treatment."

"Everything was failing. Every treatment, concoction, soup of antibiotics. Fail. I was brought in to find a cure like thousands of other scientists. And you said, 'fight fire with fire'."

"I don't remember that," Anise said.

"Well you did. The sickness was a manmade weapon, it was synthetic and it hit me that only a synthetic antibiotic could beat it."

"I know synthetic antibiotics exist. Surely you tried them?"

"We did, but we hadn't tried the specialized synthetic antibiotics. They're created through an invention here at Pitt. It uses AI to determine what will beat it. It goes through every possibility and creates something if it doesn't exist."

"AI was outlawed years ago. Federal and forty-four states. In Pennsylvania it's illegal."

"Yeah, it is. But the system was never dismantled here because so many senators were fighting to reverse that law and a new home for it had to be found."

"Thank God it wasn't. So now that you're a criminal of science what are you gonna do? Now that you have the cure."

Trent shook his head. "Nothing. It's a little too late."

"Nonsense. With nearly four hundred million people in the United States you really think everyone is dead?"

"Dead or dying?"

"Was I dying?"

"Yes."

"You didn't give up on me. Out there people aren't sick, but they will be. We just have to find them."

"You're right. You're absolutely right. Rural areas. Places really isolated may not have it." He stood.

"Where are you going?"

"To make medicine. When you're strong we have work to do."

"We?"

"We. You have something better to do?"

"Better than saving people?" Anise smiled. "Absolutely not."

<><><><>

Queens, NY

The drive didn't take long. In actuality, had Ellis and Ossie not had a car, they could have walked.

It took less than fifteen minutes to arrive on Ossie's street.

She didn't say much and neither did Ellis. He supposed they were both thinking the same things in the silence of the car. Their families.

When Ellis realized how vacant the world was, for the first time he started to worry.

Maybe it was just New York, but a part of Ellis knew that was wishful thinking.

Ossie lived in a residential area, a flat street lined with houses on both sides. The lots weren't very big, each house had a small yard and looked similar.

There were a lot of cars parked on the street, like a Sunday afternoon when no one was working.

It was eerily quiet, no movement.

One thing Ellis noticed about each and every house was the presence of sheets or towels hanging from a visible window.

Every house had them including Ossie.

They pulled up to her small, story and a half, red brick house. The blue sheet hung from the second story alcove window just above the green awning over her small porch.

She had a fenced in tiny yard and a Big Wheel was just left of the walkway.

Ellis parked in the street and turned off the car.

He looked over at Ossie who stared out the window. "Do you want me to go in first?" he asked.

She shook her head. "Ellis, what do the sheets mean?"

"I don't know. Every house has them."

"You think it means people are sick."

"Maybe."

Ossie shifted her eyes to Ellis, sadly pursed her lips and opened the car door. Ellis did the same, staying a few feet behind her.

He would be there for her for support.

Ossie opened the screen porch door and reached for the handle of the inner door. "It's not locked," she said.

"Maybe looters. Let me open it."

"Oh, Ellis." She shook her head. "I don't care."

The very second the door breached the frame opening a little, Ellis knew. So did Ossie.

She groaned when the smell they both were all too familiar with wafted their way.

Turning his head before going in, Ellis took a deep breath to hold. More than anything he wanted to cover his mouth, but a part of him thought it would be disrespectful, because he knew her family was in there, or at least one of her two children.

The living room was empty, no one was there. A staircase was to his left and he could see the kitchen from where he stood by the door. The sun poked through the bright yellow curtains, the low hum of buzzing flies filled the air.

Immediately, Ellis opened the living room windows.

"I'll check the bedrooms," Ossie told him.

"I'll come with you."

"No." she held up her hand and walked across the living room and through an archway.

He assumed that was the way to the bedrooms.

He walked toward the kitchen and straight to the window above the sink.

Empty bottles of water were on the counter next to half a case of unopened ones. Dried up old soup was in the pot on a stove. Dishes stacked high in the sink and various ones all over the counter, medications were everywhere. On the kitchen counter were papers, print outs of stories, call logs, notes and flight information all spelling out to Ellis that they had been searching for their mother.

The house needed air. He opened the window then the back door. It was then he heard a sob come from the bedrooms.

His heart dropped and he lowered his head.

Ellis thought about going to Ossie. It took a few moments of courage and he decided to go against her wishes and find her.

But he didn't get to step from the kitchen before she sauntered in, barely able to move her legs.

She collapsed into a chair at the kitchen table.

"I'm sorry, Ossie. Let me get you some water." He walked to the sink and grabbed a bottle, opening it for her. "I am very, very sorry." He handed her the bottle.

She took it and set it down and glanced at the papers. "They were looking for us."

"Yeah, they were."

Ossie released a single sob.

"So where do we go now? Tell me." Ellis asked. "You said your daughter lived here, what about your son?"

"No need." She raised her hand. "They're here. My daughter is in her room. My son and his wife in the other. They were born in this house and they died in this house."

"Oh, Ossie. Ossie." Ellis reached for her.

She didn't react to his touch, only staring down. Then Ossie slowly lifted her head, speaking softly and without emotions. "Now may I die?"

Hearing her say that was a physical shock to Ellis, causing him to retract his hand and step back. "What?"

"May I die now?"

"Ossie ..."

"Ellis, I have nothing left. No one left. I'm done."

Ellis nodded slowly. "I understand why you feel that way and where you're coming from. This is tragic and is making me question what I am going to face. Maybe it's wrong, but I won't stand here and talk you out of it, tell you why you shouldn't. That's not fair to you and if you truly have your mind made up, is there anything I can do?"

Ossie only looked at him.

"It's your choice, Ossie. I just can't be here when you do it, so I'll leave you alone. Just know I don't want you to. I really don't want you to."

"Thank you."

Ellis leaned down and kissed her on the cheek, squeezing her hand. "My friend," he whispered. 'It has been a privilege to know you." He stood up straight. "Thank you." Ellis turned and stopped, looking back at her. "Ossie, know that I could not have done anything without you. You kept me going. You were there for me and I will forever be grateful for having had you in my life. You'll never be out of my mind or ..." he brought his fist to his chest and tapped where his heart was.

After giving a gentle smile, Ellis turned and walked from the kitchen, into the living room and out the front door.

The moment he stepped outside his heart sunk to his stomach, he wanted to scream and cry, run back in there and tell her, "I can't do this alone."

But he wasn't taking that choice from her. Her desire to live or die had to be her choice, not one brought on by guilt.

Ellis knew his best bet was to keep going and not look back.

Down the walk, through the gate, Ellis then arrived at the car.

Squeak.

Slam.

Thump. Thump.

A screen door opening, shutting and someone stepping on the porch, those were the sounds he heard.

Before he could turn around, he heard her call out.

"Ellis!" Ossie yelled for him.

Ellis looked back.

"Wait. Please wait." She walked to him. "You can't do this journey alone. No one can." She grabbed his hands. "Can you wait until I grab some things and we'll go together?"

Ellis didn't verbally reply, he grabbed her and embraced her.

"I'll wait as long as you need," he told her.

"I won't be long. You've worried so much about me and my family," Ossie said. "It's time I go with you to find yours."

TWENTY-FIVE – WHAT NOW?

Baldwin, PA

Deke sat by the living room window, staring out, thinking of a plan. He hated being in the living room for any other reason other than fear of looters.

It smelled.

Some sort odor, like horrible rotting garbage was seeping through the door. He could smell it, the same way he could always smell when Bebe's neighbors made tacos. Didn't matter where you were in the living room that smell always came through.

He remembered Bebe spraying and spraying because the taco smell got a weird scent to it after a few hours.

It was the same way, only he wished for the tacos smell instead.

That he could deal with.

He found Bebe's stash of spray and would hit it every hour. It did little to help and so Deke retreated back to the bedroom.

However, he needed to be in the living room because that window was the only way he could really see what was going on outside.

It went from mayhem to quiet and still. He could no longer see an orange, glowing sky from fires in the distance or smoke. The gunshots and shouting had stopped.

Bebe's car was out there.

They had to go the next day, they had to leave the apartment.

Two bottles of water, one juice box, four Ritz crackers, two of those tuna in a pouch things, a handful of Cheerios and a can of gravy.

If it was just him, he'd be able to stay another day or two but Ginny spit out the tuna and didn't eat the crackers. In fact, her mouth was so dry they were causing her to gag and choke.

They had ramen noodles. Two packs.

Deke got really good at making them without cooking. He remembered one time their electricity went out and his mother soaked the noodles in cold water for fifteen minutes, added ginger dressing and some cooked shrimp from the freezer.

Not that he liked that meal, but it remained in the back of his mind that he didn't need heat to cook ramen.

Two packs.

Two meals.

Two days.

But Ginny was crawling now, she reached up for the bowl that they were soaking in and tipped it over. Deke could have saved the noodles, but she crawled all over on them squishing them into the carpet. They had to have dinner, so he made the last pack.

Now they had to go.

If he could make it home, he knew he'd be able to get food. That meant he had to drive all the way there. He couldn't walk. His body was still too injured and sore.

Deke didn't see any bad people outside, but that didn't mean they weren't there.

The next morning they'd have to take a chance, he'd have to pack his sister up and leave. Even if it was to only find one of those help centers.

People still had to be there.

For the time being as he stared out the window, he thought about how to drive. Deke knew he could start the car, he just had to remember all the things he watched his parents do when they got in the car.

He wished he would have asked more.

Deke was confident, sort of, that he could do it.

What choice did he have?

<><><><>

Holly River, WV

Jen stood from a crouched position in front of the fireplace. Her knees ached a little from the change in weather and being in a squat position for so long.

She dusted her hands then grabbed the fire poker. "My thighs will feel all this squatting tomorrow. This should be good enough for tonight," she spoke to herself. "Save on some candles."

A lantern perched on the small kitchen table next to the defrosting pack of meat. She had several still in the freezer. She was just happy she thought to crank the freezer up to the highest level. Sure everything was iced up, but it would take a while to defrost.

Thinking about what she could do with the ground meat, burgers crossed her mind and she went to the freezer, opened it quickly, and pulled out the buns. After she took what she needed out, she replaced the others. Time was running out on the perishables.

It was getting late, the sun had set, then again, it was fall.

Just as she started getting items to make dinner, she heard the knock at the door.

"Come on in, Monty."

The door opened with a creak. "How'd you know it was me?"

"Ha," Jen shook her head. "And you just in time. I'm gonna make burgers."

"Want me to fire up the pit with the grate."

"That would be awesome," she replied. "I mix them, you make them?"

"Deal," Monty said. "Got the fire going. Flute open?"

"It is." She turned around finally and saw he was holding the phone. "Did you get a call?"

"My dad got the sat charged enough. It was spotty and I had to freaking run up the road and call him back."

Jen winced. "Sorry. I know it's cold."

"That's okay."

"What did he say?" Jen asked.

"After bitching about how bad and dirty my car was for three minutes?"

Jen laughed.

"He's about an hour outside of Queens. He knew what route to take."

"So he'll technically be back tomorrow?"

"Yep." Monty nodded. "Maybe, depends on survivors and if he has to help them."

"Can I ask you something?" Jen walked to him. "And you don't have to answer this."

"Okay."

"Is he always this selfless?"

Monty laughed. "Not really. I mean to us kids, yes. This is a bit of a shock to me. Why do you ask?"

"Just ... do you think he knew?"

"About?"

"YPP-234. I watched the trials, he denied it, but returning to the quarantine, it seems a bit of a guilt move."

"Like Josh?" Monty asked.

Jen nodded.

"So you are asking if my father perjured himself, knew all along about the weapon, but then felt guilty because it got out?"

"Um, yes," Jen said reluctantly.

"Yeah," Monty nodded. "I do, too."

<><><><>

Queens, NY

Ellis passed a sign. It didn't register to him, but it would. It would tuck itself in the back of his mind and it would come in handy.

Medical Camps can be located at Retail Lots.

He passed that sign two blocks before he saw a huge set up at the Big Giant Grocer. Tents, cots out in the open, military trucks. The street beforehand had been blocked off, but he and Ossie drove through. There was no one to stop him.

Ossie gave him directions to go around the main roads, just in case traffic was bad.

"People are going to try to leave the city," she said.

"And go where?" asked Ellis. "I mean, I get it, I do, but where are they going to go?"

"If I were to pack up, I'd go to a small town. Somewhere off the path, away from other people."

Ellis nodded. "You know maybe that's where people are alive."

"Even if they're not. It's the place to go. The big cities, big towns, too many bodies."

"That's assuming it's everywhere."

"Ellis," she sighed out his name. "Look around. Have you seen anyone?"

Sadly, Ellis shook his head. "But, that doctor in Pittsburgh is still alive, right? I mean it wasn't that long ago that he sent that message. He's isolated like we were. He's alive and has the cure."

"For who?" Ossie asked.

"For anyone still alive that needs it."

They spoke a little bit and then Ossie directed him to the street that would take them to the main road. They had to get on it to get across the bridge.

But it was shortly after they made the turn that traffic was stopped.

Cars upon cars lined up, making a third lane on the exit to the highway. Not one of them was running, some car doors were open. But it was packed and there was no way to move forward.

"What now?" she asked.

"How far is it across the bridge?"

"A couple miles."

"There's got to be a car on the other side somewhere, right?" Ellis shut off the engine. "Let's take our supplies and the gas can and we walk. We have the flashlights, it's getting dark, but we can make it."

"Ellis, with all those cars it's going to be a nightmare."

"I know. But we have to try. On the other side, somewhere, we'll find a car and get through this. Ready?"

Ossie nodded and reached for the car door.

<><><><>

Staten Island, NY

Bad music, bad odors in Monty's car, pretty much whenever General Scott was in the vehicle it was just bad. Not to mention the bag of marijuana in the car. Not that Scott would judge one on marijuana use, after all he himself tried a little pot in the days before he joined the service.

But he was responsible, he didn't leave it hanging around.

The only luck Scott really had was syphoning gasoline. It was plentiful, too many people were home sick in bed.

Scott took a lot of back roads for precautionary measure, but didn't have a choice when it came to the last leg of his journey.

After a bad satellite reception call, Scott ran into more bad luck.

If he wanted to get to JFK Airport located in Queens he had to go through Staten Island, which was already getting thick with traffic when Scott had left.

Sure enough, the road was blocked, there was no way to the airport by going through even on sides streets. He either had to get a boat to cross the bay or walk the bridge.

He opted for the latter.

Scoot could have gone north, but it was too far out of the

way.

After securing the car in a place he could retrieve it, Scott gathered some items and began to walk.

<><><><>

It was bad and much worse than Ellis expected.

As they moved deeper into the crammed packed traffic, the less empty the cars were. Ossie whimpered so much and with every step.

"Don't look," he told her. "Just keep walking."

"It's everywhere. How can you not look?"

She was right.

There was no way to avoid seeing the bodies in the cars and trucks, some hanging out the window, some dying on the road by their vehicles.

Where were they going with such desperation?

Were there that many cars that there wasn't enough road to hold them all and traffic came to a halt? If so, how far did it extend?

Maybe there was a road block.

The bridge across the bay was the most frightening thing of it all.

There were two directions of traffic. All cars were headed to Staten Island as if that were a safe haven.

In his mind, Ellis had a plan. Stop for a few hours and rest because of the dark, but it was too scary. All those bodies, the smell and the empathy he felt for their fear.

Despite the darkness that fell upon them, they had to keep going.

Ossie started to move slower.

"Do you need to stop?"

"No. I can't. At the other side of the bridge we may find a place to stop. Not here. Not now."

Ellis understood. He also was hit with a desperate slap of reality as he crossed the bridge. His hope of finding his family alive and well was dwindling.

If all those around him didn't survive, what were the chances his family was alive.

Ellis tried not to think about that. He really did. He needed to get home to Bebe and his kids.

Every time he thought about a negative fate for them, he countered it with them being in Pittsburgh.

That doctor was alive.

Maybe Pittsburgh was fine.

"Hello!" a man's voice called out. "Hey!"

Ellis stopped and looked at Ossie. "Another survivor."

"You don't think he's going to rob us do you?"

"I didn't think of that," Ellis replied, then heard the running footsteps coming his way. "Here. Take this and hide." He handed her the gas can.

"Where. Hide where?"

"Get behind a car. I'll try to fight them off."

"Be careful," Ossie told him.

Easier said than done, Ellis thought. He was not a physical fighter. Not one bit. Now if his friend James were there and alive, James would fight. He talked all the time about how he was a boxer.

Then Ellis saw the man coming his way. He had short gray hair and he was older. That worked in Ellis' favor. Ellis had the age advantage if he attacked. But the guy was pretty big.

Then as Ellis braced for a fight or attack, he realized the guy looked familiar.

Where had he seen him?

The man caught up to him and caught his breath. "Sorry if I scared you," he said. "My name is Montgomery Scott, I'm a general ..."

"You were on the TV, the hearings for the weapon."

"Yes. Yes, I was." He placed his hand on his hips. "And you were on the plane that was quarantined."

"I was. How do you know?"

"I recognize you from the cameras. I watched you all every

day. Twenty-three B, Ellis, right?"

"Yes. Ossie, come out," Ellis called to her. "It's safe." Ellis looked back at Scott. "What are you doing here? You obviously left the hangar."

"I did. I was chasing someone infected."

Ossie replied as she approached. "It didn't make a difference did it?"

Scott shook his head. "I was on my way to the hangar. To get whoever survived. Are there more of you from quarantine?" he asked.

"We are what's left," Ellis said. "A few others, but they went their own way. The others died. Even those working there, stationed there, the doctors and stuff."

Scott facially expressed his sorrow at hearing that. "So is there any reason for me to go there?"

"Unless you're looking for information about the cure," Ellis said. "But the power went down. That's actually how we got out."

"There is no cure," said Scott.

"That's not what the doctor in Pittsburgh said. He sent a message right before the power went down. He figured it out."

"Pittsburgh. Trent Bonoski. A scientist at the university. Rebecca was communicating with him. He's alive?" Scott asked.

"Yesterday he was. That was when he sent the message. And if he has the cure, he's not going to be dead."

"I know exactly where he is," said Scott. "I can help you find a car or get you a lift. Might not be a good idea to drive on the roads at night, but we can leave first light. Where are you folks headed?"

"Pittsburgh," Ellis answered.

"To find Doctor Bonoski and the cure?"

"No, to find my family," replied Ellis. "But if the cure is there, I'd like to find him as well."

"Well, good," replied Scott. "I'll take you both. This way to my car. It's not that far." Scott reached out and took the bags from Ossie and turned, leading the way.

Ellis wheezed out in relief.

There was some hope.

And for the first time in a long time, he really believed he was finally going home.

TWENTY-SIX – TO BE SAVED

Baldwin, PA

It was time to go. Deke had removed everything he had blocking the door except the one table. He left it there while he got Ginny ready. Just in case.

Whether he was scared or not Deke knew they couldn't stay in that apartment any longer. The smell was becoming horrible and after looking out the peel hole, he knew it wasn't good.

He saw a body lying in the doorway of the apartment across the hall.

He was still in a lot of pain, but he had to suck it up. He only needed to make it down to the car with the baby. His young mind feared being pulled over by a police officer and getting in trouble, it didn't cross his mind that nobody was out there to arrest him.

There is nothing to carry, but the baby. No food, no supplies. Only Ginny and her sippy cup which was half full with a mixture of water and the left over bit of the juice box.

Even though he didn't need the carrier, he took it just in case they had to walk. Deke strapped it to his body. It was hard twisting his arms to get it placed on correctly. He put Ginny inside, her back to his chest.

He dressed her as warmly as he could and found the car keys.

"It's time to go, Gin-Gin. We'll be alright."

He darted a kiss to the top of her head which was just against his chin and walked to the door. He just had to move the table and undo the bolt.

As he reached to slide the table he heard and saw the door knob turn.

Whoever was on the other side jiggled it then tried again softly.

His heart went to his throat, silently whimpering, "Oh no, not again."

Deke was scared. They were so close to getting out of there.

Bang.

Whoever was in the other side was trying to break down the door.

The noise caused Ginny to cry which in turn caused an increased intensity in the attempts of the looters to break in

Bang. Bang.

He watched the door rattle. It was so loud. They would get in for sure.

Obviously someone figured the apartment wasn't empty, so Deke did the first thing that came to mind.

Tried to scare them. Maybe it wasn't the smartest thing but he had to try.

"Go away!" Deke shouted over the pounding and Ginny's screams. "I have a gun! I'll shoot."

The pounding stopped.

"Deke?"

Deke lost all breath, a rush of hope and relief slammed into him. "Dad!"

"Deke!"

"Hold on." With excitement, Deke moved faster than he had in days and raced to the door. He shoved the table away and unlocked the bolt.

When Deke flung open the door, with a crying baby in his arms, he saw his father. Even though at that moment behind his father was a big, older guy and woman, Deke saw only his father. Before his dad could make it through the door, he was embracing his son and daughter.

"Oh my God, Deke, Deke," his father wept. "Ginny. Oh,

sweetie," he kissed them both then pulled back. 'What happened to you?" he placed his hand on Deke's face, then took Ginny from the carrier.

Deke shook his head. "It's okay. I'm so glad you're here, Dad, I was so scared."

"I know. These are my friends that helped me get to you. General Scott and Ossie."

Deke looked at them as he stepped back to allow them all to come in. "Dad, we ran out of food. Bebe and Dennis were sick, they got on some bus like over a week ago. Mom, Daryl and I haven't talked to anyone." He started to cry. "Then these guys came in here, took everything, they ..." His head hung low.

"I am so sorry you went through that."

Ossie stepped to him. 'You are so brave, your mother is proud. May I clean your wounds? Please."

Deke nodded then glanced to his father. "We have to find them, Dad. We have to."

"We will. But first, clean up and we have to get you out of here." He embraced Deke. "We'll find them."

Deke absorbed the feeling of his father's hold. Even though it hurt, and it physically hurt him a lot, Deke wouldn't trade that embrace for anything in the world.

His father made it back.

Deke and Ginny would be fine.

<><><><>

After finding himself apologizing again for the state of his son's car, General Scott was even more embarrassed when he saw Ellis' ex-wife's house.

Of course he wasn't too embarrassed when he saw Ellis' wife's car. She and Monty could give each other a run for their money.

But someone had syphoned all her gas and so they packed into Monty's car.

"My mom has cars," said Deke. "A couple big ones in the

garage. I know where the keys are."

It was a short drive and General Scott hoped the boy was right. They were cramped in Monty's car and they hadn't figured out what was next.

Then they pulled up.

Scott had never seen a home quite like it. A newer home on its own lot, set way back from the road and near one of those 'every house looks the same' housing developments. This home stood out. To him it reminded him of a miniature Downton Abby house.

When he commented on that Deke relayed his mother was a huge fan.

It was just amazing, the long driveway that wrapped around. A huge four door detached garage.

The home looked phenomenal.

Scott offered to go in first to make sure it was okay. The last thing he wanted was Deke to go in and see his mother and stepfather deceased.

Deke gave him the key and Scott knew as soon as he walked in there weren't any bodies.

It smelled sort of stale, like a home closed up for vacation. He took time to look in each room and there were a lot.

There was evidence someone was sick. One of the bedrooms had an unmade bed, some blood was on the pillow case, water bottles and medicine was strewn everywhere. The room also had a sour smell.

Locking it from the inside, Scott closed the door.

Every other room was fine and untouched. Food was still in the pantry and cupboard, the fridge food had spoiled.

After opening up some windows to let fresh air in, Scott went back outside to deliver the good and bad news.

No one was dead inside and no one was home.

When he said the house was empty, he saw the look on Deke's face.

Sadness, disappointment.

"Let's get inside and get you some food," said Scott. "There's plenty of it, just don't open the fridge. It's pretty bad."

Deke nodded and walked inside.

"This is a beautiful home," said Ossie. "My whole house could fit in a third of this. Less."

"It's a bit much," replied Ellis as he closed the door.

"Dad." Deke turned around. "We have to find them. We do. We can't just forget about them."

"Deke, we will," Ellis assured him. "You said they took a bus."

"Bebe did, yeah."

"Do you think your mom and Daryl took a bus, too?"

Scott cleared his throat. "I bet Deke could tell us what car is missing. I don't think they took a bus. By the looks of this house they probably drove."

"My stepfather was sick," said Deke. "And I know hospitals weren't taking people. If they were sick they had to go to the medical camp."

"Son," General Scott said. "There were several per city. They may have even gone to another area."

Deke whimpered. "How are we going to find them?"

Ellis replied. "One place at a time. We'll check one place at a time. Each bed if we have to."

Ossie gushed out, "Oh, Ellis, you cannot take Deke with you. He can't. We were at that quarantine. It was horrible. If he doesn't have to, he shouldn't see it."

Deke defended. "I'm almost fifteen. If my mom is sick, or Bebe, I need to find out."

"You will. But God forbid it's worse," Ossie said. "And if they are gone, it's not the last memory you want of them. Trust me, please trust me. Ellis, I will stay with the children while you search. The baby needs a bath and fed."

"Dad, no, I can go."

"I know, but Ossie brings up a point. I spent a lot of time moving bodies," said Ellis. "And going camp to camp, it's a lot."

General Scott spoke up. "We may not need to."

Ellis faced him. "What do you mean?"

"I know that all the official medical camps were keeping the names of all those that were sick, what symptoms they had and when they came in," Scott replied. "It was hastily planned, but it was still implemented. Find a way to keep track of everyone so families can locate each other when it's all done. The registry was updated hourly and probably did so until the power went down. Deke said Bebe left while there was still power. Which means, if she and Dennis, even his mother are at an official camp, which if they took the bus they are. We can look in the registry for their location."

"I don't think the government was expecting this outcome," said Ellis. "You really think they registered everyone?"

Scott nodded. "I do. What does it take to type in a name and date of birth? They probably were registered right on the bus."

"Yeah, but how do we find this registry? Ellis asked.

"Every research center and medical camp has access to the registry," Scott said. "I think before we search for a needle in a haystack or go camp to camp, we kill two birds with one stone. We go to Bonoski, he had the registry and you said the cure."

Deke gasped. "There's a cure?"

Ellis nodded. "Supposedly, yes."

"Dad, then go get the cure. If they're still sick you can give it to them," Deke said.

Scott responded. "That's what I'm thinking. And fortunately for you guys, Bonoski and his lab are in this city."

"University of Pittsburgh," Ellis said.

Ossie shook her head. "That campus has to be huge. I mean, how will you find him?"

"I have a great memory," Scott said. "I remember an earlier message conversation between him and Rebecca where he said he was helping out in the medical camp outside of his lab. I deployed troops to help out there. Terrance Street, Oakland? Do you know where that is?"

"Actually, yeah, I do," said Ellis. "I had one semester there. Let's go."

"We can do that, but get your family situated and comfortable first," said Scott. "I'm finding a better car."

TWENTY-SEVEN – UNCOVERED TRUTHS

It was another case of 'ditch and walk' or rather park and walk. There was no way General Scott was going to abandoned that eighty-thousand dollar SUV with a full tank of gas. He parked it to make it look like it was abandoned in traffic.

Ellis got them into Oakland, taking a lesser known route over the river and coming in the back way.

Then like everywhere else, traffic blocked the way.

In fact they parked not far from a medical camp, but it wasn't the one they needed.

"I suppose," Ellis said as they walked. "There are probably several out this way."

"How far are we?"

"Oh, like three blocks," replied Ellis. "See those buildings up the hill, That's Terrace Street."

"Maybe we'll find another way and I can go back and get the car in case Bonoski has a lot of stuff."

"I doubt it. We're pretty close."

It didn't take long, keeping a brisk pace, they were there in ten minutes. But it was a war zone. The camp was set up in the street and spread for as far as the eye could see.

Tents and cots were everywhere. Military vehicles were abandoned.

There were bodies every square inch.

Before they even arrived at the camp they could smell it. It was a something Ellis claimed he knew well but would never get used to.

"Forgive me if I don't talk," said Ellis. "I'm gonna throw up."

"Don't swallow the saliva. Push your tongue to the roof of your mouth."

"Will that work?"

Scott shrugged.

"Why did they do this?" Scott asked. "I mean, come here to die. I would have stayed home."

"Maybe they thought they'd get the medicine they needed." Ellis spoke through his hand covering his mouth.

"It's heartbreaking, it really is. The government should have been forthcoming about how bad this would be. How there is no hope."

"We're here because of hope." Ellis stopped walking. He looked left to right.

"What's wrong?"

"Do you have an address?"

Scott shook his head.

"Well, it's one of these four buildings. Which one?" Ellis pointed. Three tall glass buildings and one small round one.

Hands on hips, Scott peered around, then snapped his finger. "I have an idea."

The slight thump and rattle of the box being set on the counter caused Anise to raise her eyes from her map to Trent.

"Done already?" she asked.

"Well that box. I think we can do one more box and, that's it. The ingredients are low and I just filled the generator again."

"How long do we have?"

"Five or six hours," Trent replied. "Right now we have enough to save two hundred and twenty-four people."

"So the next and final batch could bring it up to three hundred?"

Trent nodded. “At least. How are you doing mapping out our road tour?”

“Well.” She paused to sip from a cup. “We have several options. I think our best bet is West Virginia. You want rural, that’s rural.”

“What about Kentucky?”

“Are we really gonna pass right through West Virginia and not see if people need help?” She set down her mug. “Can I ask you something?”

“Sure.”

“Is it over? I mean can people still get this?”

“I don’t know. But I am working on the assumption that the spread has slowed because it’s reaching the smaller areas. We’ll do what we can. That’s all we can do.”

“Doctor Trent Bonoski,” A voice called from outside. A deep voice. “Calling Doctor Trent Bonoski. Are you there?”

“Is it my imagination,” Trent said. “Or is someone really calling my name over a loud speaker?”

“Sounds that way.”

“I’ll be back.”

The windows didn’t open, not unless Trent broke them, so he walked from his office lab, through the halls and down three flights of stairs. All the while his name kept being called.

Stepping out of the building, he saw them. A bigger, military looking man standing on the hood of a truck with a megaphone, and a thin guy who needed a shave staring up at him annoyed.

“Are you looking for me?”

The military looking guy, lowered the megaphone and jumped from the hood. “Doctor Bonoski.”

“Trent,” he replied. “Call me Trent. Who are you guys?”

Ellis replied. “I’m Ellis Ridge. This is General Montgomery Scott.”

“Oh my God, I know that name,” said Trent. “Rebecca, she mentioned you. How is she?”

“Dead,” replied Scott.

“Oh.” Trent was taken aback.

"Doctor Bonoski. Trent," Scott said. "You sent a final message to Rebecca saying you cured this. Did you?"

Trent just stared for a second, then turned and waved his hand. "Come with me." He then led them to a building on the other side of the street.

It reminded General Scott of a murder mystery movie. A library café with a hidden door behind a shelf of books probably no one ever read. It led to a large room with a humming generator, a hulking mechanical structure eight feet tall and at least eight feet long. At the end of that was a huge computer set up with two monitor screens.

"This is where the magic happens," said Trent. "I've been manufacturing doses for a couple days."

"So it does work?" Scott asked.

"It does." Trent heard the 'oh wow' come from Ellis and looked over to see him sit down at the computer. "Hey, don't touch anything."

"I'm fine," said Ellis. "This is what I do. Computers. Software."

Trent grunted some in irritation, then pulled out his phone. "Look." He scrolled through showing the image to Scott. "This a picture of Anise five days ago. She was dying." He switched photos. "This is her this morning."

"Remarkable. So this is where you are manufacturing the doses?"

"Yes, but I'm running out of ingredients. I'm going to take what I have and see if I can help people."

"You still didn't say how you came up with the cure. Was it a fluke?"

"No it was ..." He looked over at Ellis again. 'I wish you wouldn't touch that. You're gonna break it."

Ellis waved him off.

Trent continued, "It was remembering this." He pointed. "Or

that."

Scott was confused for a second, then it hit him. "A computer."

"Not just any computer. A computer designed to find a cure and treatment for anything by breaking down the invader or virus and finding out what defeats it. It's brilliant, and I was so deep in the illness and traditional methods of finding a cure, I forgot about it."

"Wait. How does a computer figure it out?"

Trent answered. "AI. Artificial Intelligence."

Scott's eyes widened. "AI is illegal."

"Uh, yeah, duh," said Trent. "Why do you think it's hidden? A brilliant system that probably could have cured all types of cancer inside five years and it's hidden in a room from the board game Clue. Shameful. Because it was that fast and that easy."

"What do you mean?"

Trent walked over to the computer. "I just fed in the info and seriously, it took a few minutes. Bam. Cure. AI is that good."

"It's not just AI," said Ellis at the computer. "The schematics and programming has to be done by humans. AI isn't just born. Not yet, that's why they made it illegal so it would not reproduce itself. That's why I had to design my weather module the old fashion way. Now something in here had the info already.'

"No." Trent shook his head. "The computer is that brilliant. Designed by sixteen of the world's greatest medical and scientific minds."

Scott shook his head. 'All this and it happened too late. Too bad the world's greatest minds didn't think of using their invention."

"Most of them are dead. But yep. Two days," Trent said. "The medical camps got over run. Or maybe I would have thought of it."

"Well, we have it now. Speaking of having something," said Scott. "Do you have access to the last updated Medical Camp registry?"

"I can pull it. Are you looking for someone?" Trent asked.

"A few people."

"Okay, it's in my office across the street. Let's go." He glanced again at Ellis. "Can you leave that alone?"

"Um, yeah," Ellis swiveled his chair. "I found the designers. They're the ones that contributed Intel to this, right?"

Trent nodded. "I guess, why?"

"This name. Why does this name sound familiar?" Ellis pointed. "J. Brayden."

"J. Brayden." Scott rushed over. "Joshua Brayden. Is that saying he contributed to this?"

Ellis nodded. "Yeah. Who is he?"

"Only the guy that created YPP-234."

"Holy shit," said Trent. "No wonder it came up so fast. YPP-234 components were already in there."

"Wait. Wait." Scott held up his hand. "The man who claimed there was no cure, who acted as if there was no way to beat it, not only contributed his ... whatever recipe to this machine, he knew about it?" He grunted. "Are you serious? All along he knew."

"Maybe he forgot." Trent shrugged.

"He didn't forget. He knew. That fucker."

"Whoa." Ellis turned his chair. "Whoa. Hey now. Language."

"Language?" Scott raised an eyebrow. "You're not upset about this because I sure as shit am?"

Ellis winced. "I'm very mad. But you don't see me cursing. You lose all argument the moment you swear. Remember that."

"And do you preach forgiveness, too?" asked Scott sarcastically.

Trent chuckled. "This actually is a very welcome moment of humor for me."

"Well, I'm not laughing," Scott said. "I wasted my compassion on that man. If he wasn't dead, I'd kill him myself."

"He's in there." Ellis stood. "His footprints are all over this program. And I only just started. But you know, it seems rather moot now. So, Doctor Bonoski, you have the cure, you're making the medicine. Help me find my family now."

TWENTY-EIGHT – BRING THEM HOME

Waiting on Trent to come back with results on whether or not he found Bebe and Dennis was entertaining for Ellis.

He gave the doctor all the names, including Tammy and Daryl, plus a few friends. Trent seemed happy to help.

The man looked tired and worn, he definitely needed to bathe or at least wash. The older woman Anise who was ill was exceptionally cleaned up. Especially since Scott asked her to come with them.

She loved the idea but really wanted to help Trent take his road trip and deliver the cure.

It was funny watching the interaction between Anise and the General. She called him Montgomery, not Scott or General like everyone else.

"I think that boy needs me," said Anise. "He can't go looking to help people alone."

"Ma'am how about we discuss this when he is ready to go? You may not want to. I am willing to go with him. For now, we are going to a house to hash things out and set a plan. Ellis' ex-wife has a mansion that is decked out."

"Alrighty," she replied. "Let me go get ready. Trent got me some clothes and things I needed. He is so nice."

"Yes, he is ma'am."

She was already dressed and she carried a purse that snapped like something the Queen would have carried. In fact, she had it with her constantly.

After she left the office, Ellis asked Scott. "Do you think Trent got her that purse, too?"

Before Scott could answer, Trent did.

"No," Trent said. "She came in with it. I remember my grandmother with her purse and she was very particular about keeping it close to her. Here." He handed Ellis a manila folder.

"Here you go," Trent said.

"You found them?"

"I did. All of them," Trent replied. "Your wife, son, ex-wife, those friends of yours. The husband, Daryl. Nothing."

"My son, Deke said Daryl was one of the first ones sick."

"Then he probably died at home or in a regular hospital," Trent said. "I do know if he had this, he didn't survive it."

"Thank you." Ellis opened the folder. "This was last updated two days ago. But it's just names, dates of birth and location and some numbers. No status."

"No, it's just the registry. The number is their registry number. When it was taken."

"This is a five digit number," Ellis said in shock.

Trent nodded. "It was bad."

"Wait. Tammy is with Bebe and Dennis?" Ellis read. "No Daryl. How did they end up together? Their numbers are sequential. They were together."

"Don't sound so shocked, Ellis." Scott walked over to Ellis. "You have a close extended family. As soon as Anise is ready, we'll head out, get Deke and find them. Do you recognize the locations?"

"I do." Ellis read the sheet. "James' parents are in a Monroeville camp which is close to here but about thirty miles from their home." He lifted his eyes to Trent. "Was there no rhyme or reason to where they went?"

"They filled up fast," Trent replied. "How far is your wife from her home?"

"Not far. She's at a camp in Bethel Park. Not far at all from where we lived." He inhaled with a shiver. "Do you think they're there? I'm not asking if you think they're alive or dead. I don't even want to think about that right now. But could they have moved them?"

"No."

Scott peered over Ellis' shoulder and pointed down with his index finger. "What is the DC next to the camp name? Is that FEMA? Washington run? I don't recall seeing that."

"When's the last time you saw the registry?" asked Trent.

"Early on," said Scott. "Over a week ago."

"That makes sense." Trent nodded. "A week or so ago it wasn't there. DC," he said. "Dead camp. Meaning it was given that when eighty percent of the camp was dying and or dead. I'm sorry." He looked at Ellis.

"Thank you," Ellis replied. "But I am not going to allow myself to be heartbroken yet." He closed the folder. "Not yet."

<><><><>

It was something Ellis and Deke had to do alone. While he reiterated to General Scott, he didn't mind if he came along, he just preferred finding Bebe, Dennis and Tammy by himself, it was something private.

General Scott understood fully, plus there were things he said he needed to do with Doctor Bonoski. Ellis figured they were plotting their road trip for healing after General Scott checked in with his son in hiding.

Ellis knew exactly where the medical camp was located. He also knew that being midafternoon, it could take days going through that camp until he found his missing family.

He was ready for it.

Emotionally, he did prepare himself for the worst knowing that was the more likely experience.

He had medication though, courtesy of Trent, just in case some were alive.

He exchanged the fancy SUV that Scott preferred to a pickup truck, just in case he had to bring his family back.

After taking the back roads, Ellis arrived to the area. The

only reason they were able to get close was because traffic had stopped but a bus lane was clear.

They drove in the new bus lane until they arrived at the end of a line of busses.

They didn't have far to walk at all, and if need be Ellis could have driven farther, but he wanted to take a moment to prepare his son just one more time.

Right before where the medical camp was supposed to be was a health building with doctor's offices and physical therapy. That parking lot was full and Ellis parked there, using the half a block walk as time to talk to Deke.

Outside the truck, Ellis stopped Deke.

"Are you ready for this?" he asked his son.

"I am Dad."

"Look, I know you want them to be alive. I do, too. But we have to both be ready for what we may find."

"I hear the silence," said Deke.

"What do you mean?"

"The silence. The noises, crying shouting. I know what that means. But I have to know. Even if it's to say goodbye."

Proud.

Ellis was so proud of Deke. He still felt incredibly bad about how much his son had endured. The pain, the fear. And now, again, his son was taking on more than someone his age should have to.

After giving Deke a hug, they began their ascent into the camp.

The bus route ended at the rear of the shopping lot where a large grocery store and a Walmart were located. At the end of the lot was a closed down car repair shop. The bay doors to the garage were open and inside it looked as if they set it up as a receiving area. Long tables with papers on them, laptops, just left there.

The bodies of two men were on the ground. Both had PPE suits, but their head gear was off.

Ellis went into that garage and easily found masks and

gloves for him and Deke. If they were looking for Bebe, Dennis and Tammy, they would be going through a lot of dead bodies.

At least that was what Ellis thought.

He didn't realize the massiveness of the task they were about to take.

Not by judging the area around that garage. Nothing else but parked vehicles were in that side and rear portion of the lot, perhaps that was why it was such a shock when they turned the bend.

Deke had to stop.

Not because he was scared but because the enormity of the medical camp was overwhelming. Every square inch of the parking lot was covered with open tents with cots, it even looked as if they ran out of cots and people made beds on the ground.

There was an orderly fashion to everything, but it was evident that it got ahead of the people taking care of the sick.

Half the people had IVs, they all looked as if they were receiving care, but one thing was certain, there was no movement.

No sound.

And a horrible smell. Much like the one that came into the apartment. Deke figured it had to be the dead.

"Ready?" Ellis asked.

Deke nodded and moved forward with his father.

The only thing he really hoped was that his mom, brother and Bebe weren't on the ground. Tossed aside, suffering on the concrete when they could have been home in bed.

They walked east to west, from the building to the street and back up.

It was hard to look at each body and Deke, avoided any that were large and male. His insides shuddered with each small person under a blanket, fearful it was his baby brother.

The large tire shop was a standalone building, unlike the Walmart and grocery store which were connected. Between the tire shop and grocery store was a side parking lot.

It took over an hour, but they finished looking at every person that lost their lives to the plague and were in front of the tire shop. They still had seventy-five percent of the lot to search.

But when they got to that side lot, the section between the buildings, Deke heard his father gasp.

"Oh, God," Ellis groaned. "Don't let it be there."

Slowly, almost fearful, Deke looked to his right.

There weren't cots in that side lot or tents. There were trucks parked four across and Deke couldn't see how deep.

All of them were packed with bodies.

As brave as he had been, the sight of all those bodies, there had to be thousands, it was too much for him.

Deke knew things were bad, he watched it all end from the window of that apartment. He felt the desperation of mankind when those men came into the apartment, heard the cries and screams, but the finality of what happened hit him right there.

The sight of those trucks was a blow. Deke wanted to scream, cry. His body shook, his face tensed up.

"Dad. I can't."

"It's okay," Ellis said. "It's okay."

"I can't." At that second, Deke didn't feel like a teenager. He felt like that little boy again that ran from the Easter Bunny at the mall.

An emotional flight or fight.

Deke chose flight.

It was instinct, he spun, muttered out an, "I'm sorry." And ran. Not back to the truck, the garage or toward the rest of the parking lot filled with the sea of bodies.

He ran straight, darting around the canopy tents that sheltered the sick from the elements.

But Deke didn't make it far.

Two tents from where the end of the lot met the fast food restaurant, Deke stopped.

He didn't turn around, he just backed up.

Ten paces.

How did he even see? He was moving so fast.

But he did.

When he stopped, he turned his head.

An uncontrollable ache seeped from his throat and it wasn't a sound of joy. It was one of pain and instant agony.

It was a vision of the final moment between the two women he loved most in the world and the little brother, he loved and adored.

The two cots were joined, side by side, not an inch separated them. One blanket covered them all. Dennis was on his side in a fetal position, nestled in his mother's hold. Bebe's arm draped over him and Deke's mom faced Babe and Dennis, her hand holding on to Bebe.

They were gone.

For as much as Deke wanted to scream and run to them, he couldn't.

He just collapsed to his knees right there at the end of the cot.

Ellis knew.

He gave it a few seconds before he chased after Deke, allowing his son to get it out of his system, but the second he saw Deke stop, back up and drop to his knees on the ground, Ellis knew.

He ran to his son, calling to him breathless from fear.

"Deke." Ellis arrived at his son. "Deke."

He was afraid to look, he really was. But if his fourteen year old son could, Ellis had to.

It was sight he would never erase from his mind and heart.

There was a sense of peace and love, but also pain between Bebe, Tammy and Dennis. Holding on to each other in their final moments as if to say, "We're here for each other."

What he did in that instant upon seeing them, Ellis didn't remember. It was a blur. He froze perhaps.

The most intense pain he ever felt in his life flooded his body and soul. He lost his wife, but worse than that, he lost his child.

He wanted release from the agony in a form of a scream, but didn't.

Instantly, Ellis gathered what strength he could and dropped to the ground to hold Deke.

Their emotional goodbyes, final touch to Bebe, Dennis and Tammy would come.

The decision of what Ellis and Deke would do next would come.

For that moment though, they just cried.

TWENTY-NINE – FOR THE LONG RUN

The home was magnificent, General Scott just wished he was there under circumstances that weren't so tragic.

He stood in the kitchen that morning, staring out of the sliding glass doors. The view was phenomenal, he felt like he could see for miles.

Scott could also see every level of the yard that probably cost close to fifty grand if not more to landscape. The party garden had a barbecue station, grill and bar any backyard chef would die to cook on.

The next level was a pool, and the final level a yard.

This was now a tragic view, that was where they buried Ellis' wife, his son and Deke's mother.

He watched the three of them, Ellis Deke and Ginny stand by the graves.

Ellis kept thanking Scott and Trent for preparing the graves.

It wasn't a problem for Scott, it was the least he could do.

The enormous amount of pain Ellis was going through, losing a wife and child, Scott knew all too well. His own son Monty could relate to Deke.

Different situations, but all the same pain from the loss, Scott was reliving it watching the Ridge family.

"Morning, General," Ossie's voice drew his attention when she came through the sliding glass doors.

"Morning Ossie."

"Come down to the garden for breakfast please," she said and went to the pantry.

"Ossie, you didn't need to make breakfast. You cooked for all of us last night."

"It keeps my mind busy." She came from the pantry with syrup. "Please. Come down. I made coffee."

"Coffee. Oh I'm there."

Ossie went back out and after a beat and another glance down to Ellis and his children, then Scott followed.

Anise sat next to Trent at the table on the garden patio, while Ossie placed food down.

"Morning." Scott said pulling out his chair, "How are you feeling, Anise?"

"Oh, I'm doing much better," she said. "Almost full strength. That baby gave me some energy."

Ossie set down a cup of coffee for Scott. "Tell me about it. That Ginny is a blessing. Eat General."

"Thank you, Ma'am you're too kind." Scott glanced at Trent who was focused on the contents of a folder. "Everything okay, Doc?"

"Yes." Trent looked up. "Just thinking. I know I wanted to go rural. West Virginia, Kentucky, but I only have enough medicine to save a few hundred people. I need ingredients to make more and I need to get them."

"Where are the ingredients?" Scott asked.

"Cleveland."

Scott nodded. "Well, the computer isn't going anywhere, neither are those ingredients. Why don't we see if we need to make more?"

"I get that, but there are other medications that machine can make. Fresh. Eventually what is on the shelves at the pharmacies will expire."

Ossie said as she sat down. "A bridge to cross when we get there." She grabbed a pancake from the stack and began to slice it in small pieces.

Anise asked. “Is that for the baby?”

“It is,” Ossie answered.

“You think they’re too big?”

“They’re fine.”

“She’ll choke.”

“They’re fine,” Ossie said stern.

Scott cleared his throat. “Anyhow, when Ellis and Deke join us ...” he paused when he saw them approach. “Never mind, they’re here.”

When he reached for a chair, Ossie offered to take the baby. He handed her over and sat down. So did Deke.

“What did you need us to join the table for?” asked Ellis.

“I needed to talk to everyone,” said Scott. “First off, it’s an honor to be with you all. There’s not much out there and we need to stick together.”

“Agreed,” Ellis said, reaching for coffee.

“I would like very much after I check on my own son, to hit the road as soon as possible with the doctor to look for people in remote areas that may need help,” Scott said. “But I also think winter is just around the corner. As great as this house is, I believe we need to establish a foothold somewhere that is self-sufficient. We’re drinking bottled water here and using what is left in the tank to wash. That won’t work in the long haul.”

“Why not?” asked Deke.

Ellis answered. “While we don’t need electricity or gas to live, we need a place that is sustainable. This isn’t it. A place designed to be, well, off the grid.”

“When?” Deke asked.

Ellis answered. “Probably the sooner the better. If we survived, others did and they may not be so nice.”

“I know that.” Deke lowered his head. “I’ll go wherever you go,” Deke replied. “I just don’t understand why we have to go to an off grid place. Is there a need? Isn’t everywhere off the grid now?”

“Yes, in a sense,” Scott said. “But we need to focus on you and your sister. The young. The future belongs to you and we have to make sure you are there to steer it. Yeah, right now the world is our grocery store. So much still on the shelves, and we will need it until we can handle things on our own, but we don't want to be some apocalypse tv show where they're still eating canned pasta ten years later. It doesn't work that way."

Trent asked. "Are we going to search for a place while we're out there?"

Scott nodded. "We will. We'll search. Maybe we'll find a town when we're out there. Some place already established that will take us in. In the meantime, if you guys are open to it," he said. "When you're ready to go, I have somewhere we should go in the interim.

THIRTY – STAY

Holly River, WV

Jen hadn't seen him all morning, but she heard Monty. She knew he was working on the project he started a few days earlier.

It was cold and had rained the night before, she was ready to kick herself for not bringing a heavier jacket, but she never thought she'd be there when the weather took a turn. Now it looked like it was going to be a while before they got off the mountain.

She took the road down to the main entrance to the camp area. Past the pool and the playground. It was the entrance to an old church, a gazebo, country store and office. It was right at the entrance, the only entrance which was off of a narrow single lane road.

Monty had finished.

He had taken that metal arm that blocked off the campsite during off season and built a large gate. Not that it would stop people from walking around it, but cars couldn't go through.

"Hey," she called out as she made her approach. Just about there, she saw the Sat phone on the ground. Monty probably charged it again using their generator. She lifted it. "Hey."

Monty stopped hammering.

"You think you have enough nails in there?" she asked.

"It's done. Just thinking about the next one. The next project."

"And that is?"

"Well, if we end up settling here, I'd like to find a way to make the gazebo a green house."

Jen laughed. "For real?"

"Yeah."

She nodded. "Sounds like a fun winter project. I mean, we'd need supplies. Not sure anything around here would work."

"Yeah, so we'll do it as a winter project. We're stuck anyways."

She handed him the phone. "Anything?"

"Not even a signal." He dropped the phone. "The world is dead."

"Oh, Monty."

"No, Jen. We need to face that."

"I don't believe the whole world is dead. Whenever we get down from this mountain, you'll see that. We talked about that, you know." She nudged him. "Going out and seeing if anyone is left, if so, do we join a community or come back here?"

"Moot point. Since we no longer have a car. My car. I loved that car. He took my car."

"Monty."

"It was lived in, but mine. Messy, but mine."

"I know."

"It's gone. There are memories in that car, not to mention cool PT clothes I stole from my dad."

"There are more important things," Jen stated.

"But you need a car to get to them," Monty said. "It's a long walk in the cold."

"We can stay until the weather breaks, or your father shows up."

"He's not showing up," said Monty. He bent down and gathered his tools. "I think he got sick. He's not coming."

"Monty, I think you need to give him time. It's only been a week. Have faith. He's done so much, he's gonna beat this."

"I don't know." His head cocked when he heard a car horn. "Someone's here." He moved for his tools and grabbed a revolver from the tool box.

"Monty," Jen scolded. "What the hell?" she walked to the gate. "Let them in."

"What if they're looters?"

"They wouldn't beep." Jen reached for the gate, she pulled it, but it wouldn't budge.

Monty walked over and undid the latch, opening the gate after he did so.

Jen smiled. "You were saying about your dad."

Monty grinned as his father stepped from the SUV. "Dad." He rushed to him.

Scott gave his son a huge hug. "Great job here."

Jen stepped closer. "I'm Jen."

"Ma'am." Scott held out his hand.

"Oh, please." She scoffed and hugged him. "Your son is my life saver."

"Mine, too," replied Scott.

From the embrace, Jen saw a truck behind the SUV and two men, two older woman, and children got out of the vehicles. "People."

"Yep." Scott nodded. "Brought you some company. We figured we'd get them here before the weather gets bad. It's a good place. We brought supplies, too."

Jen watched each person pass through the gate and she greeted them with a smile and nod. It was good to see them. They looked lost, sad and tired. She wanted to tell them 'welcome home' but thought for right now it would be too much.

Scott introduced everyone to Jen and Monty.

"Your children?" Jen asked Ellis.

"They are," Ellis answered. "My son and daughter."

"Oh, I am so happy for you. I'm glad you have each other."

"Thank you," Ellis replied.

Scott turned to Jen. "Can we find them all places?"

Monty answered for her, "There are enough cabins."

"Good. Again, Monty," Scott said. "You did really well here."

"No, Dad," Monty looked at the people. "You did really well. I'm proud of you."

"Thanks. Now," Scott patted him on the back. "Why don't I

get these folks back in the vehicles and drive them up …" He stepped back.

"One … more thing." Monty held up a finger, and his father stopped walking.

"What's that?" Scott asked.

Monty looked left and right. "Where's my car?"

THIRTY-ONE – EPILOGUE

Holly River, WV

Ellis had spent most of his life between Pittsburgh and Buffalo and swore he had never seen snow or storms quite like the ones that were hitting the mountain. He stared out the window in the small cabin, watching the snow come down hard again for the third time in a week.

It started right after Christmas and seemed to never stop.

He sighed. "I can't believe how deep it is. I bet it's three feet now. I can't even see the step to the porch."

"Ellis," Ossie snapped. "If you are gonna go, go. If not, take off that coat and boots."

"Oh, leave him alone," said Anise. "You're always picking on him."

"I am not."

"Am, too."

"Drink your tea."

"Cover that baby's head it's cold," said Anise.

"She is not an infant, she is fine."

Ellis smiled and turned away from the window. Both women sat in chairs by the fire place. Ossie had Ginny on her lap.

Ginny loved them both and in the four months that they had been on the mountain, the two woman, fast became friends but fought like an old married couple.

"Not to pick on you like Ossie," said Anise. "If you don't go down and make a path, they aren't coming back tonight and you'll be stuck with us."

"Fine." Ellis took his knit cap from his pocket, put it on, then his gloves and lifted his hood. He stepped out onto the porch

The handle to the snow pusher rested against the railing.

When Ellis stepped down to get it, he realized the snow wasn't as deep as he exaggerated, but it was still deep.

Using the snow pusher was going to be difficult, but not as bad as it was four days earlier when he waited too long.

They had one.

He wasn't sure why that was and they all shared it. It wouldn't have been so bad if they all stayed in the cabin area, but Deke, Monty and Jen worked that greenhouse they put together. They were always there and if Ellis didn't create some pathway to them, all road markings would be buried and walking back would be dangerous.

It wasn't a short distance to the green house. They couldn't build it closer to the cabins because the cabins were surrounded by trees which would have shaded the green house.

Ossie and Anise shared the biggest and nicest cabin. It was the first one in the circle community. Cabin ten had the huge kitchen and both women took it upon themselves to do the cooking. Their cabin however, wasn't protected by trees and was an honest representation of how much snow had fallen.

And it was a lot of snow.

Ellis moved that push plow slowly because it felt as heavy as pushing a car. Giant snowflakes fell and every gust of wind was bitter and biting. He looked back over his shoulder and saw the rising smoke from the chimney. He debated on going back to the warmth of the cabin.

But he trudged on.

The entire past few months had been nothing but trudging on. He was good at that push plow and snow removal, Ellis hated that those were his top talents in a post apocalypse world.

However, it wasn't as empty as they all thought.

Scott and Trent were constantly on the road, looking,

searching, reporting back. They never said much about what they came across just that staying on the mountain was the best thing to do for now.

The last time they checked in and took a break was Christmas and right before the snow came, Ellis recalled the conversation.

Anise was adamant, "I think you should go south for this leg of the trip. Won't be long. It's gonna be a tough winter here. I can feel it."

Scott looked at Ellis. "What do you think?"

"Why are you asking me?" Ellis asked.

"Aren't you a weatherman?"

Ellis laughed. "Hardly, I designed a weather program, I don't know weather. I worked at Panera."

He believed they trusted Anise more, but Ellis didn't know. They were actually unpredictable.

It took a while, snow to his shins, and he arrived at the Gazebo. And there was Monty right on top of the high structure.

They ended up just using the frame of an old shelter to make the greenhouse instead of the large Gazebo. It was more than just a Gazebo, it was huge and it probably was once used for big parties. Now it was the place where they put the radio antenna. It was perched on the roof, the line ran down to the kitchen, which was now the radio room, and it was powered by a generator.

The green house was right next to it. The plastic was foggy and he saw the figures of Jen and Deke.

He looked back up to Monty and yelled. "Get down! It's slippery and you're gonna get hurt."

"What?" Monty replied. "I can't hear you. The wind is too loud."

"I said get down!"

"Hold on I'm coming down."

Elis grunted and plowed his way to the green house. He rested the plow handle against the door frame, and shook off as much snow as he could before entering.

There was a big temperature difference when he went inside, they were probably running the heater. It didn't take much to warm it up.

Deke was with Jen across the green house working on something.

She had been a godsend, Monty as well, they helped Deke more than Ellis could. Monty through his own life experiences and Jen with her teaching skills and patience. Ellis really thought she was a good woman. Although he cringed every time she spoke fondly of her husband Josh and the wonderful things he did.

With his passing, Doctor Josh Brayden was canonized a saint in his wife's eyes, much like most families do when a member passes.

To Ellis he was a monster. Yet, no one ever told Jen about what Josh Brayden had done. How one man's greed inadvertently led to the end of the world, and worse, somehow conveniently forgot there was a way to cure it pretty quickly.

It was a debate on whether to tell her or not. Then Trent brought the argument that Josh didn't intend for it to happen and if he really did remember about the AI tech to bring the cure, there was no way it could have even helped enough people before YPP-234 spread its terror. It moved too fast, the computer couldn't make enough fast enough. Maybe Josh knew that and opted to get people comfort and help. Trent estimated that because of air travel, before Josh was brought in, it had already spread.

Ellis didn't buy it. Some people wouldn't be dead, like Ossie's grandchildren. The man that could cure it was right there.

But it wasn't his call to shatter the illusion Jen had. Who was Ellis to tell her that? For all he knew Jen was already aware, after all Monty probably knew and he was a stoner with a big mouth.

Ellis kept quiet about Josh to Jen.

"You guys ready?" Ellis asked. 'Anise said it's gonna get bad and if you don't come now you won't get back."

"Hey, Dad," Deke said. "Did you do a path?"

"I did."

Jen smiled. "You are so good with that."

"Yep, we all have our dystopian talents. Pack it up please." His eyes shifted to three potted plants that looked as if they were failing. "Guys, how many times do I have to tell you that you can't grow marijuana in here at this time of year? Let alone that it's illegal."

Deke tossed up his hands. "Not me. Him." He pointed.

The door opened and Monty walked in. "Are we done for the day? Why is Ellis here?"

Ellis replied. "Not to witness my underage son tending to illegal plants."

Monty laughed. "It's not illegal. I think that law went out when the plague hit."

"It'll be back, trust me. People want to hold on to their morals."

Monty snorted a laugh. "You're so funny with that freaking stuff."

"Language."

"I didn't swear."

"The intention was there."

"Oh my God," Monty laughed. "I'm so sorry Deke."

Shaking her head, Jen grabbed her coat. "Any luck with the antennae?"

"It's hooked up," replied Monty. "I'd like to monitor it for a bit, I'll catch up with you all later."

"Are you sure?" Jen asked.

"Yeah, I want to see if my dad checks in."

"Not long okay?" Ellis said. "And let us know what they say."

"Of course. See you at camp." Monty put his hood up and backed out again.

Ellis watched him walk back to the gazebo and into the kitchen door. He hoped there would be some news, but there never really was anything new. Ellis felt they were sheltered from more than just the elements and General Scott was being secretive as a means of protection.

Ellis was a big boy, he could handle hearing anything.

But he and the others were safe and had what they needed, he guessed that was all that really mattered.

"Ready?" Deke gave a swat to Ellis' back. "Hey, can I push the snow plow on the way back."

"Be my guest."

"Cool." Deke ran by him, excitedly. "I'll plow us home."

As Jen walked out, she passed a gentle smile to Ellis.

He pulled the green house door closed and watched his son enthusiastically grab the manual snow plow.

Deke often used the term 'home' when referring to the cabins. Something Ellis didn't do.

The mountain wasn't home. He wasn't sure it ever would be or if there ever could be a home for him and his children.

It was a place for the moment. A safe and healthy place.

Ellis could live with that. He could live without all the snow, but that came with the territory.

Despite the fact he wasn't too crazy about his current surroundings, there wasn't a day that went by that Ellis didn't think of his losses and count the blessings he still had in his life.

<><><><>

Harkers Island, NC

"Yep, and Mr. Goodie Two Shoes was at it again," Monty's voice came through the headset speaker.

Scott laughed as he sat in the back of the van in the radio set up. It was warm and he kept the doors open. "Well, Ellis isn't really a goodie two shoes, a lot of that I think is a put on to irritate you."

"Even the 'language' thing?"

Scott depressed the radio button. "Okay, maybe that's not an act. I'm surprised you even know that phrase goodie two shoes."

"I got it from Anise," Monty said. "Everything good?"

"Yeah. Won't be much longer." Scott closed his eyes when he

said that. He knew it wasn't the truth. When they first went back to the mountain, he told them more people survived than they thought. What he didn't tell them was the sickness was moving just as fast in the west and south. They ran out of doses pretty quickly and had to backtrack north to Cleveland and Pittsburgh.

"Where are you at now?" Monty asked. "We have a good connection."

"I really rigged the van. The antenna looks like some sort of spy get up. We're in North Carolina."

"Seriously?"

"Yep. Hitting the little islands off the coast. Came on a tip."

"A tip?"

"Ran into a small group that was getting supplies, they were on a ship when everything hit and seems there are a few out there plague free. I told them in a little bit, we'll coordinate a way to bring them to shore."

"So you're in contact?"

"Oh, yeah, the monster radio van helps with that," he said.

"They should be able to come home, though, right? It's over, the plague is done."

"It's done," said Scott. "Just bits here and there."

"You'll get them."

"We'll get them. Now head back before you get snowed in and that genny runs out."

"I will. I love you. Stay safe, Dad."

"Stay warm." After telling his son he loved him, Scott set down the radio microphone and stepped out of the van.

He felt kind of guilty enjoying the sunshine while his son was battling the snow.

But Monty and the others were safe.

The van was parked outside of a church and Trent was inside with the two dozen ill. All of them seeking comfort from their sickness in the presence of their faith.

They would finish up and move on in a day or two. To another small down or island with very little population. That was where their focus was.

When YPP-234 first arrived, weaponized in a young woman, she wasn't the only one.

It hit hard and fast in the densely populated northeast United States, spreading out like spider webs everywhere. Each new town or city rejuvenated the weapon and it started again. Like a cat chasing its tail, it truly was futile to stop it.

That was why Scott and Trent focused on where they could do some good. As the months moved on, they were arriving too late. If they were able to cure anyone, it was usually only one or two. Just like the church on Harkers Island. Only one person was getting better. They needed the cure early or else it didn't do any good.

While some people had a natural immunity to it, most people did not. There was no vaccine, much like strep, just because an individual caught it didn't mean a person couldn't catch it again.

That was what made it so scary.

Trent did some testing on their core group. Trent had immunity, as did Ellis and Ossie. Scott had it as well. The others didn't catch it out of luck and staying clear and that was why Scott insisted they stay on that mountain.

Far away from civilization and safe.

He could have joined the others at the Holly River Camp, waiting it out, but that wasn't Scott.

Scott would be what he always was. A good soldier on the ground doing the work needed. Helping those who he could and comforting those he couldn't.

It was his way of seeing things first hand and knowing when it was all done, when YPP-234 finally burned out.

Eventually it would be over, like every other plague before them. Making its way through the world, touching all it could before finally disappearing. It wouldn't end the way Scott hoped, with more people surviving than not, life returning to pre plague normal. That would never happen. But YPP-234 would end. Until then, Scott would keep going. He would keep fighting to keep his family and the others safe.

He always remembered a quote he heard from Ronald Reagan. He kept it in the back of his mind and it became his mantra as he moved across the countryside with Trent. The quote was, *'We can't help everyone, but everyone can help someone.'*

At the end of the day Scott could close his eyes and know he was doing all that he could.

<><> THE END <><>

AFTERWORD

Thank you so much for taking the time to read this book. I really hope that you enjoyed it. Please know, good or bad, I appreciate hearing from you and can be reached at Jacqueline@jacquelinedruga.com.

Please feel free to visit my website
www.jacquelinedruga.com

BOOKS BY THIS AUTHOR

After The Haze

After surviving a terror attack that took her husband, Lucy is trying to rebuild her life for her two teenage children. She makes the decision to move them all to an off-grid mountain community.

Away from the insanity their life had become, their temporary solution becomes a permanent way of living. Lucy believes she is giving her kids the perfect life, and a way of living that they truly want.

Until the day her son, Vincent, decides to leave without saying a word.

Lucy and her daughter, Avery, leave their secluded life to search for him in the nearby town. But what they find is nothing short of shocking.

Everyone is dead and there is no sign of Vincent.

Soon Lucy learns that it isn't just the town of Piedmont, it is everywhere. A fast-moving phenomenon sweeps across the globe, pushing mankind to extinction and allowing only a few to survive.

Lucy pushes on in her search for her son, but can she find him before he crosses paths with the anomaly...or is it already too late?

The Black

Before the sun rose over the town of Sisterville everything went black. A natural disaster of unknown origins takes the lives of every living creature and decimates the small town.

Disgraced NASA scientist and now Cleveland Weatherman, Hero Galanis knows he is more than a local celebrity on television. He recognizes the anomaly on the satellite image as a repeat of the event that cost him his career. Decades earlier, Hero made predictions about the devastation the anomaly would cause, but those predictions pale in comparison to the reality the world currently faces.

The mysterious events are no longer popping up years apart, but now hours apart with no signs of slowing down. Nature is cleaning house and the reset button has been pressed. The extinction clock is ticking and mankind races to beat it.

The Black is a standalone novel.

Gone

Greg Benedict watches in horror as his wife and baby stand by window inside of a burning building. Then, before the flames reach them, they vanish. It was just the beginning.

Sporadic vanishings occur over the next several months, all leading to the day when half the population disappears.

Gone.

Chaos ensues as humanity struggles to come to grips with the sudden vanishing of half the life on earth.

Those who remain search desperately for answers. Some believe it is a bigger picture, the start of the apocalypse and the rapture has occurred, while others like Greg believe there is a scientific reason for it. He vows to find it and stop it.

Whatever the reason, it's not over. And oblivion to the human race, along with everything on earth is a heartbeat away.

Printed in Great Britain
by Amazon

56666236R00126